9 Bodies Rolling
(a Body Movers novel)

STEPHANIE BOND

DEDICATION

To all the fearless Roller Derby Girls who keep the sport alive.

CHAPTER 1

"AND THIS PHONE has a dual aperture camera," the sales guy said.

Carlotta Wren squinted, thinking the smart phone he held looked pretty much like the other six sitting on the counter. In hindsight, she should've brought along her tech-nerd brother Wesley to help her choose. "Um... what's a dual aperture?"

Priscilla Wren lifted on her tip toes to peer over the top of the counter. "It means you'll look better in selfies, even if the lighting is bad." The little girl smirked. "You should definitely get that one."

Carlotta pursed her mouth. For a nine-year-old, the girl had a cutting tongue.

The sales guy smothered a smile. "Your daughter seems to know her stuff."

"I'm not her daughter," Priscilla supplied. "I'm her sister."

"Ah, well that explains the resemblance."

"I'm much prettier," Priscilla said matter-of-factly.

"Prissy," Carlotta chided.

The guy laughed. "Yes, you're very pretty." Then he glanced back to Carlotta with open admiration. "And so is your big sister."

"We didn't know about each other until a few weeks ago," Prissy prattled on. "I was in hiding with my parents."

The guy suddenly looked concerned. "In hiding?"

Carlotta gave Prissy a warning glance, then coughed up a laugh.

"My little sister has an active imagination."

He seemed appeased, then pointed to the phone Prissy had recommended. "It's also on sale, a really good deal if you sign a service contract."

Ah, now he was speaking her language. "Okay, I'll take it."

"Can I have one, too?" Prissy asked. *"Please?"*

"We talked about this. Maybe when you're a little older."

Her sister pouted, but didn't argue—for once.

Carlotta turned back to the sales guy, holding up her old phone. "Can you transfer my contacts?"

"No problem," he said, taking her phone. "Plus photos, music, whatever. Do you want to stay with your same service provider?"

"Sure," she said, then glanced at her watch. "Will this take long?" Hannah Kizer was meeting them for lunch after some shopping of her own.

"Not at all." He moved toward a computer terminal and typed in her name as she spelled it. "Yes, here's your account." His flirtatious smile faded. "You're on the friends and family plan of a Peter Ashford?"

"Um... yes," Carlotta murmured. "That needs to be changed."

The guy grinned. "You broke up, huh?"

"He's in jail," Prissy supplied helpfully. "For stealing money from a bunch of rich people."

"Peter didn't steal money," Carlotta corrected her sharply. "He only... helped." In the sense he knew about the money counterfeiting scheme at Mashburn & Tully, but he didn't report it.

"Everyone blamed it on our dad," Prissy told the sales guy. "That's why we were in hiding my whole life."

The guy looked thoroughly confused, then grinned at Carlotta. "So... you don't have a boyfriend?"

"No, she doesn't," Prissy said. "And she's getting kind of old. Do you want to be her boyfriend?"

"That's quite enough," Carlotta said through gritted teeth.

"*I* have a boyfriend," Prissy said to the salesman. "His name is

Jack and he's a policeman. We're getting married."

"Wow, he sounds... older."

Prissy nodded. "But he said he'd wait for me."

"Don't hold your breath," Carlotta muttered for her ears only.

Add her little sister to the long line of women who'd fallen for Detective Jack Terry's charms, and were destined to be disappointed.

"Hello, Wren twins," came a voice behind them.

Prissy turned and grinned. "Hannah!"

Hannah Kizer sported black leather shorts, red tube top, and combat boots. She set down her shopping bag and opened her arms wide for a hug from Prissy, who ran to her.

Carlotta squashed the stab of envy over how quickly her little sister had taken to her tatted up, stripe-haired, foul-mouthed friend. In fact, it seemed Prissy had bonded with everyone new in her life—Hannah, Wesley, Chance, Jack, and Coop—more than she'd bonded with her big sister who'd found where her parents and Prissy had been living in Las Vegas under assumed names.

Still, Carlotta's chest welled with love and pride as she studied the little girl interacting happily with Hannah. Priscilla was a precocious, bright child, with a winning personality. And although she resembled Carlotta almost exactly at the same age, she was more mature than Carlotta had been. And small wonder, considering how, outside of school, Priscilla had been mostly sequestered in the house with adults, including their mother Valerie, who was, sadly, suffering from some sort of early onset dementia.

Prissy had grown up quickly.

"This nice man wants to be Carlotta's boyfriend," she told Hannah.

"Does he?" Hannah asked. "And what did she say?"

They all looked at her expectantly, including the sales guy. He was good looking, if a little young, but she wanted to laugh out loud at the absurdity of adding anything—or anybody—to her overflowing plate. "Thank you," she said, "but I'm not available."

His mouth turned down, then he shrugged. "Can't blame a guy for trying."

Hannah narrowed her eyes. "Don't tell me you're pining for Peter Ponzi-Scheme Ashford?"

Carlotta sighed. "No. And for the record, Peter didn't know about the fraud until after the fact."

"Then I hope you're not letting Jack Terry come around again? I thought he'd be too busy dealing with his crazy baby-mama jailbird Liz to try to worm his way back into your bed."

Carlotta frowned and nodded toward Prissy. "Language."

"Oh, please," Hannah said. "This girl is going on forty."

"Jack doesn't want Carlotta," Prissy said, hands on hips. "He's going to marry *me*."

Carlotta smiled at Hannah. "See? Besides, Jack and I are just friends. We made our peace before we left Vegas."

The sales guy cleared his throat, then pointed at the two phones. "I'm just going to step over there to finish this."

"Who then?" Hannah's eyes flew wide. "Coop?"

Carlotta shook her head. "Not Coop, not anyone. I'm taking a break from… men."

"Are you a lesbian?" Priscilla asked. "That would explain a lot."

Carlotta's jaw dropped. "No."

Hannah howled with laughter.

"I'm taking a break from dating altogether," Carlotta said evenly. "I've been kind of busy."

"How are things at the house?" Hannah asked lightly.

Carlotta noticed she didn't say "home"… her friend had warned her moving back into the Buckhead house where she and Wesley had grown up would feel weird, but Dillon Carver's thugs had trashed the townhome looking for the rest of the three hundred million in counterfeit bills Randolph had stolen, rendering it almost uninhabitable. She'd convinced her friend and herself she could handle being back in her childhood home.

But she wasn't handling it. Not well, anyway.

She gave a slow nod, careful not to betray her true feelings in front of her little sister. In truth, the Wren family reunion wasn't exactly what she'd dreamed it would be. The initial exhilaration of having her parents back—with the surprise addition of Prissy—had given way to the reality that the Wrens had spent the last ten years apart. What they were, it seemed, were a group of strangers with the same last name. "Great," she said. "Everything is just... great."

"Is Wes still walking on air to have his parents back?" She winked at Prissy. "And a new little sister?"

That, at least, made Carlotta smile. "Yeah... Wes is like a kid again, happy and eager to please." Seeing her brother so animated gave her strength when she felt overwhelmed. She'd hidden her mounting anxiety from him—Wesley deserved to revel in his family being reunited. "He's staying at the townhome, handling repairs. And looking after his snake, of course."

That python of his was one thing about living at the townhome she did *not* miss.

"But he visits almost every day and helps Birch with the cooking," Prissy added. "He's a really neat brother." The little girl smiled up at Carlotta as if to underline the omission that she was a neat sister.

The two of them had settled into a push-pull sistership. The one thing that convinced Carlotta her prickly little sister really did care for her was the fact that Prissy had never removed the pink plastic bead bracelet Carlotta had given her in Vegas. She even slept in it, and that said more to Carlotta than Prissy could express.

"How's all the legal stuff?" Hannah asked.

"The D.A. is still working on smoothing over Wes's charges in Vegas. But thankfully, the charges against Randolph have been dropped."

"That's the least the D.A. can do after the way he pursued your father." Then Hannah grimaced. "We were all wrong to think the worst of him."

Hannah's family had been on the list of investment clients allegedly swindled by Randolph Wren when in reality, he had been set up by his own firm.

"That's all over now," Carlotta murmured. After all, she'd thought the worst of Hannah when they were in Vegas, but the villain had turned out to be Liz Fischer.

Who was now cooling her heels in jail awaiting trial, pregnant with Jack's baby.

The notion still sent little shards of disbelief through her system. She had come so close to giving her heart to Jack... now she felt as if she'd survived a very close call, like stopping just short of a cliff. She was still swaying.

"How is your mother?" Hannah asked carefully.

Carlotta's heart squeezed. "The same. Good days and bad. She seems happy to be back in a familiar house... unfortunately, it's as if she's gone back in time to when we were all living there. But Birch is a huge help." As opposed to her father, who seemed eager to pick up his life where it had left off, sans Valerie. "And Coop is researching the best doctors and facilities for a full battery of tests."

"I guess Coop is too busy working at the morgue to do much body moving," Hannah said with a sigh. "I kind of miss it, don't you?"

Surprisingly, Carlotta was missing a lot about her former life, including the intrigue of helping Coop move bodies from crime scenes. But just thinking it filled her with guilt—she certainly couldn't say it out loud.

"Is Dr. Coop a dancer?" Prissy asked.

"Hm?" Carlotta asked, confused.

"You said he was too busy working to move his body—is he a dancer?"

"A body mover—" Hannah began.

"Yes," Carlotta cut in, giving Hannah a lethal look. "Coop dances in his spare time."

Hannah snickered, but let it go. "When are you returning to Neiman's?"

"Next week, when Prissy starts school. My boss has been patient, but it's time. Then I'll probably start spending some nights at the townhouse." She needed an occasional break from the tense atmosphere in the Buckhead house. Carlotta angled her head. "How's married life?"

"Terrific," Hannah said. "Every married couple should have his and hers apartments."

Especially, Carlotta noted wryly, when Hannah was keeping so many secrets from her stoner husband, such as the fact that she was heir to a hotel dynasty and her family was at the top of the society food chain.

"You don't live with your husband?" Prissy asked.

"Nope," Hannah said. "I have my place and Chance has his." She made a face. "That way we don't have to share a bathroom."

Prissy giggled. "Or a closet."

"Good point," Hannah said, then gestured to Prissy's orange sundress and white sandals. "Is that a new outfit?"

She nodded, posing. "Carlotta and I like to shop."

"Yes," Hannah said wryly. "I've met your sister. You two are definitely blood related."

"What did you buy?" Prissy asked, gesturing to the shopping bag Hannah had set on the floor.

Hannah grinned and reached inside. "I'm so excited... this is something I've always wanted."

"A Chloe bag?" Prissy asked.

"Givenchy boots?" Carlotta asked.

Hannah frowned. "I said something *I* have always wanted." She pulled out a box the size of a small suitcase, then lifted the lid.

Prissy's eyes went from intrigued to puzzled. Carlotta experienced a similar reaction.

"What are they?" Prissy asked.

"What do you mean?" Hannah said, lifting one of the pair out of the box and displaying it lovingly. "They're roller skates!"

"They look old," Prissy said.

"They're retro," Hannah insisted, in defense of the cream and black color scheme with stars.

"They're very cool," Carlotta soothed. "Is this a new hobby?"

"It's more than a hobby," Hannah said, puffing up. "I just finished boot camp training and I was asked to substitute on a team."

Carlotta squinted. "What kind of team?"

Hannah grinned. "I'm a roller derby girl!"

Their silence exasperated Hannah.

"A roller derby girl!" she repeated.

"What's that?" Prissy asked, looking dubious.

Hannah sighed, clearly disgusted at their ignorance. "It's where two teams of girls skate against each other to try to earn points. We have bad-ass costumes and bad-ass names and we try to knock each other down."

Carlotta bit her lip. "Are you sure it's safe?"

Hannah drew herself up. Standing nearly six feet and clad with lean, inked muscle, she looked formidable. "I can handle it."

"I was talking about the other girls," Carlotta said wryly.

"Our first match is this Saturday. Will you come and watch my debut?"

"Can we?" Prissy asked Carlotta, jumping up and down. "Please?"

At the sight of her sister's shining face, Carlotta felt her mood lift. "Sure. It sounds like fun."

"Wes, too," Hannah said. "Chance will be there."

"I'll let him know," Carlotta said, already looking forward to an excuse to be out of the house—and away from her newly-returned parents.

Minus ten points.

CHAPTER 2

WESLEY WREN paused before knocking on the door of his probation officer.

This could be tricky depending on how much E. Jones knew about the circumstances surrounding her fiancé Leonard's untimely death while Wes was in Vegas.

He pinched the bridge of his nose against a tension headache that had seemed omnipresent since returning from Vegas. Which didn't make sense considering everything in his life had suddenly and amazingly turned around. His parents were back, he had a new sister, and Meg Vincent had unblocked him from her phone.

So why had the Oxycontin cravings returned?

He took a deep breath, then rapped on the door.

"Come in," came E.'s voice.

He pushed open the door and stuck his head inside to take the temperature in the room. "Hi."

E. glanced up at him from her desk. "Have a seat, Wesley."

Brrrr. Wes closed the door behind him, then settled into the chair across from her. "How's it going?" he asked breezily.

"Fine," she said evenly, although her appearance told a different story. Her auburn hair was pulled back into a severe bun. Her green eyes were rimmed with shadows, and her cherry mouth was pinched around the corners.

"I only have a few minutes," Wes said. "I need to report to my city job."

STEPHANIE BOND

She opened a thick file. "I called your boss to let him know you won't be in today. You and I have a lot to talk about."

Wes swallowed hard. "Okay." Dammit, he'd been looking forward to seeing Meg. They had texted several times since she'd heard about his father's return in the news, but she was still being standoffish. Meg was happy for him, but he was going to have to win her over again.

"I understand from the DA's office that you've had an eventful couple of weeks."

"Yeah." He smiled wide. "My parents are back."

Her eyes softened. "I'm so pleased for you. But we need to straighten out your legal situation so you can enjoy being with your family."

He nodded solemnly.

"Let's start with the charges you managed to rack up while you were in Vegas." She read from a report. "Underage drinking, underage gambling, possession of a fake driver's license, and passing counterfeit bills." E. lifted her head. "Wow... impressive."

And yet he could tell she wasn't impressed. Wes lifted his hands. "In my defense, I didn't know it was counterfeit money."

"Where did you find it?"

He squirmed. "In the wall of our townhome, wrapped in plastic."

"And you didn't find that odd?"

"I assumed my dad left it for me and Carlotta, so I decided to spend some of it."

"You mean *gamble* some of it."

He conceded with a nod, then he grinned. "Before the arrest, I was slaying the poker tables."

"In a casino for which you were underage."

He wiped his hand over his mouth, erasing the grin.

"And apparently, you consumed alcohol while you were there."

He shifted in his seat. "A few beers, what's the big deal?"

10

She leveled a glare on him. "The big deal is how you were able to get into a casino and buy alcohol in the first place."

He shifted to the other side of the chair. "That's why I needed the fake license."

"You clearly don't realize how much trouble you're in."

Wes scoffed. "My using the counterfeit money led to the Mashburn & Tully scheme being blown wide open. Those crooks were arrested and the firm was shut down, and the drug dealer who was laundering their money is off the streets." He spread his hands. "That has to count for something."

She sat back in her chair and crossed her arms. "It does. Which is why the D.A. is trying to pull strings. But don't be thinking you're some kind of hero, Wes. You and I both know the connection to the Mashburn & Tully scheme was dumb luck."

He lifted a finger in the air. "Ah, but was it?"

She sat, unblinking.

"Okay, it was," he admitted, his shoulders falling. "But all's well that ends well, right? My parents are back home and my dad's been vindicated. Meanwhile, the real bad guys are in jail. The D.A. owes me one, don't you think?"

She arched an eyebrow. "D.A. Lucas did you a big favor already by convincing a judge to let you come home with an ankle bracelet until the charges are sorted out rather than wait it out in a Nevada jail."

He bit his tongue, then reached down and yanked the hem of his jeans to cover the device.

E. sighed. "But under the circumstances, I'm sure the D.A. will do everything he can to mitigate the charges. I understand the Mashburn & Tully operation was quite a complicated conspiracy, and your attorney Liz Fischer was caught up in it."

"Yeah... I didn't see that coming. She kind of went off the deep end."

A shadow crossed her face. "And apparently Leonard was involved."

He stabbed at his glasses. "I'm sorry Leonard got run over by a bus." He wasn't, actually. Leonard was a bully and all-around bad guy who worked for Dillon Carver, the drug-running son of the loan shark Hollis Carver, aka The Carver, whom Wes alternately worked for and against, depending on the day of the week. And he was pretty sure Leonard had gone to Vegas to kill him, so he wouldn't be shedding any tears he was gone, but E. hadn't known her fiancé was evil. "He was messed up with some bad people."

Her eyes watered. "Something I suspect you knew all along," she said lightly. "Since you were too?"

"I… probably shouldn't say."

"Wrong," she said. "I want to know everything, Wes."

He averted his gaze, then looked back and heaved a sigh. "Okay. Leonard was an errand boy for Dillon Carver, and sometimes Dillon's father. Mostly he couriered drugs, but I know he robbed a poker game once because I was there. He, um, threatened me not to tell you anything."

E.'s throat convulsed.

Wes let that sink in for a few seconds before getting to the worst of it. "Liz Fischer hired Leonard to follow Carlotta to Vegas—she was suspicious that Carlotta knew where our mother was, and she wanted to… get rid of my mom in case she could help exonerate my dad."

"That's where I'm confused," E. said. "Wasn't she your father's attorney?"

Wes nodded. "But that was a farce. She helped Mashburn & Tully to frame him because all her money was tied up with the firm."

"So if they went down, she went down?"

"Right. She's pregnant, and it must have made her desperate."

"The police said Leonard ki—" She stopped and cleared her throat. "Killed a federal agent."

Wes squirmed. "An agent was following Carlotta, too, and he had information on how she might be tracking our mother.

Apparently, he and Leonard had an altercation in Carlotta's hotel room and—" He stopped.

A tear slipped out and ran down her cheek.

"It could've been self-defense," Wes offered, although it was a moot point. Besides, Karma had caught up with Leonard—according to Chance, the thug's body had to be scraped off the street before being shoveled into a body bag.

E. wiped away the tear. "How did your attorney and Leonard know each other?" Her voice sounded slightly accusatory.

Wes pulled back. "Not through me, if that's what you're thinking. Dillon Carver was laundering money for Mashburn & Tully, so maybe Liz met Leonard through them."

She nodded, her expression dazed.

Wes's leg began to jump on its own volition. "There's, uh... more."

"What?"

He wet his lips. "A few months ago, a headless body was found." He hadn't killed the man, but he'd been forced to de-tooth the head to prove his allegiance to The Carver—an incident that still fueled his nightmares.

She nodded. "I remember—the man was finally identified, wasn't he?"

Thanks to him and Coop. "Yeah... but the murder was unsolved."

"Was?" she asked.

"I wasn't a witness to it, but I was told by someone who would know that... Leonard killed the man for Dillon Carver."

She inhaled sharply.

"And that's what I told the police." Jack Terry had been happy to close that case file, and Wes had been equally happy his buddy Mouse was off the hook.

E. looked stricken. She pushed to her feet and turned her back to stare out her office window.

Wes was quiet for long minutes, unsure what to do. "Are you

okay?"

She turned her head toward him, then her body. Her chest rose with a deep breath, then she nodded. "Yes… I mean, I will be. I apologize for the professional lapse."

"No need," he said.

She reclaimed her office chair, seeming to have crossed some mental hurdle. "So… your parents are back?"

"Right," he said, adding a smile.

"And how's that going?"

He nodded. "My father is recovering from being stabbed while he was incarcerated." Liz had been behind that incident, too.

"And you have another sister?"

He grinned. "Yeah—Priscilla is nine. We call her Prissy, and man, is she ever. Mom was expecting her when she and Dad went into hiding."

"So now your entire family is reunited."

"Uh-huh. They're living in the Buckhead house I grew up in. Carlotta is staying with them until they're settled."

"You're not?"

He hesitated, then shook his head. How could he explain that after years of dreaming of a reunion, it wasn't quite what he thought it would be? "I'm staying at the townhome and fixing it up for me and Carlotta."

"You must be over the moon to have your parents back."

He nodded. "Absolutely."

E. squinted. "You don't seem that happy."

"I am," he assured her, still nodding.

She was silent.

"It's just that…"

"What?" she prompted.

He shifted in his chair. "My mother… she's having memory problems." An understatement—his own mother didn't recognize him, still thought he was a nine-year-old kid off playing somewhere. A lump of emotion rose to the back of his throat.

E.'s brow furrowed. "I'm sorry to hear that. I'm sure all of this unwanted attention has been quite a shock to her system."

He swallowed hard. "Yeah, reporters are hanging out in the bushes around their house. The police try to keep it clear, but they ring the doorbell at all hours."

"I'm sure your family will be the subject of public scrutiny for some time. It's quite a story."

"Unless you lived it." It was as if now that his parents were back, he was supposed to forget about the years they were gone.

E. leaned forward, resting her elbows on her desk. "And how are things with you and your father?"

"Fine," he said, trying to sound convincing. But the truth was, they were struggling with how to catch up on each other's lives when so many important moments over the last few years had gone unshared.

"Just fine?" she asked mildly.

"Great, actually," he amended. "It's going to be great." Realizing that didn't sound good either, he pulled back. "Why all the questions?"

She angled her head. "Wes, it hasn't been too long ago you were addicted to pain medication. I just want to make sure this upheaval in your life isn't going to trigger a relapse."

Was she some kind of freaking mind reader? His internal defenses reared. "This is the opposite of upheaval. This is putting things back the way they're supposed to be."

"Still, under these circumstances, I think most families would find it challenging to be suddenly thrust back together."

"Not us," he said quickly.

E. gave him a little smile. "Good."

He stabbed at his glasses. "I mean, yeah, Dad is being pulled in a lot of different directions, but as soon as things level out, we'll get to spend more time together. He's going to help me fix up the townhome."

"That sounds like a good father-son project," she agreed. "Is your family working with a therapist?"

He frowned. "You mean a shrink? No. Why should we?"

She lifted her shoulders in a casual shrug. "It might help everyone figure out a new dynamic, smooth the transition. It's just a suggestion. I'm only concerned about how this affects you and your ability to finish probation without any more hiccups."

Wes realized his heart was beating fast and his pits were moist. The urge to have a hit of Oxy slammed into him hard. He took a few calming breaths until the sensation passed, then sat back. "I'm good."

She studied him for a few seconds, then said, "Good. With your parents' and sister's return, you have three new reasons to stay out of trouble." E. removed forms from the file, and pushed them toward him. "Meanwhile, the D.A.'s office sent over paperwork that could help your cause. Let's go through it."

He half-listened as she talked, his mind spinning elsewhere. For the past ten years he'd thought of nothing more than his parents coming home and the Wrens being one big happy family again. He knew each one of them had suffered in different ways because of the separation, but especially Carlotta, who had sacrificed her twenties to raise him the best she could, with his bratty ass kicking and screaming the entire way.

Carlotta deserved to be happy. So he would keep his apprehension and disappointment to himself, and hope relations within the Wren clan improved. Substantially.

CHAPTER 3

CARLOTTA OPENED her eyes and blinked at the ceiling of her girlhood bedroom, disoriented. Was she still dreaming? Had she traveled back in time?

She lifted her head to see her new phone sitting on the nightstand, and her brain fog lifted. Even after several nights in the Buckhead house where she and Wes had been raised, she was still having trouble reconciling the past and the present. They seemed to be overlapping. She'd been certain that solving the mystery of her parents' disappearance would allow her to move forward... instead it felt as if she'd taken a giant step back into history.

She pushed to her feet and walked to the window where she used to climb down and sneak out to meet Peter after hours. The trees and landscaping were now overgrown and wild. The neighboring houses were in similar states of maturity, a reminder that everything and everyone had moved on since the time the Wrens had lived here before. She spotted a photographer creeping across the lawn, and stepped back from the window, letting the curtain fall.

Irritation spiked in her chest. She understood the interest in her family's story, but enough was enough. She retrieved her phone, called the midtown police precinct, and asked to speak with Brooklyn. A few minutes later, the dispatcher's familiar voice came on the line.

"Brook here."

"Hi, Brook, it's Carlotta Wren."

"Hey, girl. Long time, no see."

"I've been busy."

"Yeah, and your busy is keeping everyone else busy, too. Never seen so much commotion as the back and forth between the APD and the D.A.'s office over your father's case. How are you holding up?"

"Hanging in there," Carlotta said, trying to sound cheery.

"Good. What can I do for you?"

"There's a photographer in the yard of my parents' home, guess he waited until the patrol car cruised by. This isn't midtown's jurisdiction, but I don't know anyone in the Buckhead precinct. And this isn't exactly a 9-1-1 situation."

"I got you covered," Brook said.

"Thanks."

"No problem. Come see me sometime... and put a smile on Jack Terry's sour face, will you?"

Carlotta gave a little laugh. "That's not *my* jurisdiction, Brook." Anymore.

"I hear you. Be good."

She ended the call, indulged a barb of regret over Jack for two seconds, then hurried to dress, knowing she had obligations waiting. Remembering she'd promised to help Prissy and Birch paint her little sister's bedroom, she dressed in shorts and a tee shirt she didn't mind getting splattered, and tied a bandanna around her dark hair. It was still strange getting ready in her old bathroom. Each time she looked in the mirror, she expected to see herself wearing the uniform of her private high school and Peter's engagement ring. That version of herself was so far removed, it almost took her breath away. That was at least two lifetimes ago.

The itch for a cigarette was strong this morning, but she pushed it aside. She was getting good at resisting temptation.

Jack's face flashed in her mind.

Well… getting better at it, anyway.

At the door to her bedroom, she took a deep breath, hoping to dispel the rock of tension sitting in her stomach. But after a slow exhale, it was still there, where it had been since arriving back in Atlanta with her parents, Prissy, and her mother's caretaker Birch in tow. In no version of her many reunion fantasies did she consider her parents would return with another child and her mother incapacitated.

She hadn't anticipated it would be this hard.

Inhaling for reinforcement, Carlotta opened the door and padded down the second floor hallway. New furnishings had been hastily purchased, but the bones of the house were still the same, and the décor. The wallpaper and paint colors now seemed dated, and a little sad. At one time the walls had been dotted with family photos… the absence of them now seemed to mirror their poignant predicament.

As she descended the back stairs to the kitchen, she pasted on a smile. "Good morning," she said to the foursome at the table—Randolph, Valerie, Priscilla, and Birch.

"Good morning," her father said, offering her a wide smile. She wondered when it would stop feeling surreal to see him, to talk to him, to touch him.

"Good morning," Prissy chirped, squirming happily in her chair. "Birch made pancakes!"

"They smell yummy," Carlotta said. "Thank you, Birch."

"My pleasure," Birch said, ever calm and patient as her mother's caretaker. There was no trace of the man who had turned into a special ops soldier when Liz Fischer had taken them all hostage in the Vegas house and set it on fire. He had morphed back into the polite and competent man who had answered the door the fateful day Carlotta had found them. She liked him immensely and was beyond grateful he had relocated with them to Atlanta—although the man's personal life remained a mystery.

"Are you ready to paint your room pink?" Carlotta asked Prissy.

"Yes, but the paint color isn't just pink, it's called Pink Unicorn."

Randolph winked. "Nothing ordinary for our girl."

The interplay between Randolph and Prissy was special, reminding Carlotta of her own relationship with Randolph when she was young. He had been an adoring and indulgent father, and she had worshipped him, which had made his leaving that much more hurtful.

When Valerie turned her head toward Carlotta, she could tell instantly her mother was having a bad day. Valerie was lovely in a coral-colored sleeveless dress that showed off her slim figure, but her deep brown eyes were unfocused and her hand movements were jerky.

"Do I know you?" she asked.

"Yes, mother. I'm your daughter, Carlotta."

Valerie frowned and gestured to Priscilla. "That's Carlotta, too."

"I'm Priscilla, Mommy," the little girl said, accustomed to the name confusion.

"Okay," Valerie said, then turned back to her food.

Randolph shifted in his chair, his expression pinched. Then he put his napkin over his plate, and pushed to his feet, giving no indication he'd recently been stabbed and had almost died from his injuries. Slender and fit and sporting salt and pepper hair, he looked younger than his age. And he hadn't lost his sense of style—his trousers were perfectly pleated, his dress shirt crisp, his shoes Italian. "I'm heading out."

"Where to?" Carlotta asked.

"I'm meeting someone at the club."

She blinked. "You rejoined the country club?"

"We were reinstated. We bought the membership years ago. I only had to pay this year's fees. The Board waived the fees for the years… in between."

"That was big of them," Carlotta murmured sarcastically.

"Don't be like that," her father said, lowering a kiss to her cheek. "Forgive and forget—then start over."

Carlotta bit her tongue to keep from saying Randolph hadn't witnessed how his former friends had turned their backs on his children after he and Valerie had disappeared.

"By the way," he said, "a reporter from the *AJC* keeps calling my attorney. She says she's a friend of yours—Rainie Stephens?"

"Yes, I know Rainie."

"She wants me to do a televised interview."

Carlotta pressed her lips together. "Do you think that's wise? Things are just starting to settle down."

"I haven't said yes," he said, then dropped a goodbye peck on Prissy's cheek and Valerie's. "Goodbye, dear."

"Where are you going?" Valerie asked.

"To the office."

Valerie's mouth twitched downward. "Tell Liz I said hello."

Randolph froze, then his color darkened. "Have a good day, dear."

"Try to get home early," Valerie said. "I promised Wesley you'd help him with his homework."

Carlotta's heart squeezed. She was becoming accustomed to her mother's time switch—she seemed to be stuck in the period just before she and Randolph had left Atlanta to go into hiding, and Carlotta was certain living in their old house only reinforced those memories.

"Okay, dear," Randolph said, then turned to go.

"There was a photographer hanging around outside," Carlotta said.

"Thanks for the heads up," he called good-naturedly. "I'll make sure they get my best side." The door leading to the garage opened, then closed.

Carlotta marveled over how easily Randolph had transitioned into life in the spotlight.

Birch stood and stepped to the window, scanning the yard.

"I called for the patrol car to come back," she offered. "But it doesn't help when Randolph encourages them."

"Why do you call Daddy 'Randolph'?" Prissy asked.

Carlotta gave a little laugh. "I guess I'm still getting used to having him around."

"But your father isn't here," Valerie said with a sigh.

"I know," Carlotta said, patting her hand. "But he'll be back."

Birch returned to the table.

"Can I have some more of that good brown stuff?" Valerie asked Birch.

"More maple syrup?" he asked.

"Yes, syrup," she said, relieved to have the correct word.

"Of course, Valerie." He passed the syrup to her, then offered a plate of pancakes to Carlotta.

She wasn't hungry, but she took one in deference to his efforts. "Is the photographer gone?"

"Not yet. But that detective friend of yours just tossed the guy's camera in the day lilies, so he'll probably be leaving soon."

Carlotta frowned, then stood and walked through the kitchen and dining room to get to the front door. There she parted the slats of a wooden blind to peer out a side window.

At the curb sat a familiar dark sedan, and Detective Jack Terry stood with hands on hips speaking to the photographer she'd seen earlier. And from the expression on Jack's face, he wasn't wishing him well.

She bit back a smile as the photographer retreated and scooped up his long-lens camera near the mailbox.

Jack stood until the man was gone, then turned to walk back to his car.

Carlotta opened the door and stepped out. "You're not going to say hello?"

Jack turned back and as always, her pulse skipped a beat. He was a big man with wide shoulders that conjured up feelings of security and other less noble thoughts. He was dressed in signature dark slacks and boots, pale dress shirt and ugly tie, and a sport coat that covered the weapon and badge at this belt. His face was rocky and implacable. Even in bed, the man never let down his guard.

"I didn't want to intrude," he said.

She stepped forward, then stopped. She had to break the habit of walking toward Jack. "You're not intruding. Thanks, by the way. But isn't scaring photographers a little below your paygrade?"

He shrugged. "I was in the neighborhood. Brook knew she wouldn't have to explain the situation."

"That's true. I'm sure you know more about my family than you want to." She had first met the man after he'd arrested Wes for breaking into the city records computer. Since then, they'd been through a lot together, in various stages of dress and undress.

One side of his mouth twitched. "Your dad was leaving when I pulled up. How is... everything?"

"Getting sorted out."

He nodded. "Have you been able to have that Christmas you and Wes postponed?"

Jack was referring to the sad little metallic Christmas tree Wes had insisted they leave up, the gifts unopened, until their parents returned.

"Not yet, but hopefully soon. How is everything with you?" With Liz, with the baby—a son, Liz had oozed in Vegas, before she had embarked on her crime spree.

Jack looked away, then back. "Getting sorted out."

The door opened behind Carlotta, and Prissy ran past her. "Jack!"

He grinned. "Hi, Prissy."

The little girl stopped close to him and gazed up with adoration. "Come in and have breakfast with us."

"Priscilla—" Carlotta began.

"I can't, Short Stuff," he said, squatting down to her level. "I have to go get the bad guys."

"There are bad ladies too," she said, obviously remembering

23

when Liz had held them hostage at gunpoint.

Carlotta closed her eyes briefly. As if Jack needed to be reminded.

"You're right," he said gently. "But there are more good people than bad people—remember that."

Prissy nodded solemnly. "Are you still having a baby with that bad lady?"

She and Prissy had run into Jack and Liz together at the Eiffel Tower experience in Vegas, and Prissy had noticed her baby bump.

Carlotta rushed forward to rescue him, putting her hand on Prissy's shoulder. "Let's let Officer Jack get back to work." Her phone rang and she reached for the clip to release it. Cooper Craft's name came up on the screen. She saw Jack's glance bounce to it as he stood, and the merest smile appeared.

"Tell Coop I said hello," he said, then turned to walk back to his car.

"Bye, Jack," Prissy shouted. "Don't forget about me!"

"Don't worry," Jack called back, encompassing them both in his glance. "I couldn't if I tried." He opened the door and climbed into his car, fired the engine, then pulled away.

Carlotta sighed, then connected Coop's call. "Hi, there."

"Hello to you, too," Coop said, his voice warm and mellow. "How are you on this beautiful day?"

She glanced up at the cloudless sky and observed the mild breeze lifting her hair. She hadn't even noticed. Carlotta smiled into the phone. "Better now that you've called."

"I'll take that," he said with a laugh. "Seriously, am I interrupting anything?"

She glanced at Jack's retreating vehicle. "Not at all." Then she turned back to the house, shepherding Prissy along. "What's up?"

"I've been making calls to local neurologists, and I think I've found the right doctor to take on your mother's case. Is Valerie available next Thursday afternoon?"

"I'll make sure of it."

"Okay. I'll text you the info. And I'm happy to come along if you think it will help."

She smiled. "I'd like that, but only if you're not busy at the time."

"Deal. By the way, I'm also available to meet you outside of a doctor's waiting room if you ever just want to hang out sometime."

Carlotta gave a little laugh. "My time is pretty limited these days... but I'm taking Prissy to watch Hannah in a roller derby match Saturday night if you'd like to meet us there."

"Hannah is a roller derby girl? Why am I not surprised. Sure, sounds like fun."

"Good. I'll text you the details."

"Okay... see you soon."

Carlotta ended the call smiling. Coop was like that—easygoing and just... easy. When she had been in Vegas, her search for her mother had taken her to a coffee shop bathroom with walls covered in handwritten signatures, good wishes, and confessions of people passing through. On a whim, she'd written the name of the man she should marry—Dr. Cooper Craft. It had been a surprise even to herself considering at the time she was still smarting from Jack's betrayal with Liz, and newly-engaged to Peter.

But in hindsight, maybe her subconscious was onto something.

CHAPTER 4

"KEYS AND COINS in the bowl," the security guard at the entrance to the city building intoned to the civilians and employees lined up to get inside to pay bills, to vote early, or to slog away at their government jobs.

As part of his community service sentence for breaking into the courthouse database and canceling speeding tickets for himself and a couple of friends, Wes had been assigned to work in the very department whose sloppy coding had allowed him access to the data in the first place, Atlanta Systems Services—ASS for short. He emptied his pockets and mentally told the people queued in front of him to hurry the hell up.

He got to see Meg today.

When he left for Vegas, he was in the doghouse bigtime because he'd had to reveal he was the father of Liz Fischer's baby. That had turned out to be untrue, but the damage was done. Still, he'd had the forethought to leave a rose gold bracelet around the neck of the Georgia Tech teddy bear Meg kept on her desk. The gesture had been enough to break the ice while he was in Vegas vacationing in jail. He would try to build on that blatant suck-up move.

The guy in front of him set off the alarm. Low groans sounded all around. Everything stopped while he doubled back to walk through again, setting it off again. Wes sighed and muttered under his breath. After what seemed like hours the man discovered a wad of keys in his pocket, and the line resumed.

Wes practically ran through the detector, but was brought up short by a strong hand from behind. "Hold up there." Only then did he realize he'd set off the alarm, too.

"I'm going to need for you to go back through," the guard said.

Frustration zinged through Wes's chest.

He patted his shirt and pants pockets frantically for forgotten items, but came up empty. The guard waved him through again… and again the alarm sounded.

"Step over here, sir," the guard said, leading him to the side, but still in plain view of everyone else.

He assumed the position to be wanded. The guy waved the baton detector up and down Wes's skinny body, then stopped when it beeped—by his ankle. In a flash of horrified realization, Wes remembered the ankle monitor that had allowed him to leave Vegas while his charges were being considered. At the moment, however, it didn't feel like a gift.

"Sir, I'm going to lift your pant leg," the guard said.

Wes sighed. "Go ahead."

The guard yanked up his jeans to reveal the thick black strap that secured to his ankle a flashing box the size of a pack of cigarettes.

"Ah, your ankle bracelet set it off," the guy said.

"I forgot I was wearing it," Wes mumbled. "Sorry."

"No problem," the guard said, studying the device. "That's not a Fulton County monitor."

"Nah—it's a souvenir from Vegas."

The guy grinned. "Vegas, huh? Was it worth it?"

"Yeah," Wes said, puffing up. "Totally."

The guard laughed heartily, then finished wanding him. "Okay, you can go on through, Vegas. Just speak up next time."

"Will do." Wes turned, then balked to see Meg standing there. His mouth went dry at the sight of her. Her dark blond hair was corralled on the top of her head in a sexy, messy knot, and she was wearing a pink dress like she'd invented the color. But she was not smiling.

"A souvenir from Vegas, huh?"

He swallowed hard. "Uh... I can explain." Meg knew he was on probation for tampering with courthouse records—he'd been able to spin the hacking incident into something that sounded vaguely cool... but he'd been hoping to keep the Vegas incarceration from her.

She narrowed her eyes. "Does this have something to do with your father's situation?"

"Yes," he said quickly. "Yes, it does. I was... following clues my dad left and I... got in a little trouble." Then he gave her a convincing smile. "But the D.A. is going to fix everything."

She softened, but looked dubious. "Are you sure?"

"Hell, yeah. My dad's a freaking hero, and the D.A. owes my family bigtime for making him look guilty all these years."

She bought it, nodding. "Okay... good. Because I'm not dating a guy with jail jewelry."

His heart buoyed crazily. "We're dating?"

"Not yet. But I'll keep you posted." She wheeled off and walked ahead of him, her dress swishing, leaving him in a wake of her fresh, citrusy perfume.

He jogged, trying to catch up to her. "How do you feel about roller derby?"

"Politically speaking, I'm in favor of it," she called back. "I think it empowers women."

"My friend's wife Hannah is skating on a team Saturday night... want to come watch?"

Meg stepped onto the crowded elevator and when she punched the button he saw she was wearing the bracelet he'd given her. "Maybe," she called as the door was closing. "Text me the info."

He smiled to himself and texted the info to her. They were *so* dating. He headed for the stairwell and bounded up several flights of stairs. He was leaning against the wall whistling when the elevator door opened and she walked out.

For the charmed smile she gave him, he'd run up a hundred flights.

"I'm glad you're back," she said, goosing his ego. They fell in step together. "Your dad's story is all over the news, Wes. You were right about him."

He grinned. "Toldja."

"I know. You must be overjoyed to have your parents back."

Except they weren't really 'back,' more like "nearby." "Sure."

She squinted. "Just 'sure'?"

He recovered. "Sure, I'm overjoyed…. absolutely. It's just kind of surreal, you know?"

Her eyes went all dreamy. "I can't imagine… it's like a movie, complete with a secret baby!"

"Yeah, just like that," he agreed.

"Tell me about your mother."

He hesitated, unwilling to share his mother's condition. "She's… the same." Technically true since she seemed stuck in the past. "Still pretty and classy."

"I'll bet she can't stop hugging and kissing you," Meg said.

Since he was a stranger to his mother, notsomuch. His first attempt to hug her had been traumatic—she'd thought he was attacking her. The most interaction they'd had since were cautious handshakes at arm's length. "Of course," he lied.

"What's your new sister like?"

"Just like my old sister, except shorter."

That made her laugh, a tinkly sound that had every man in the department peering over the top of their cubicle.

She's mine, schmucks.

"Maybe I'll meet them all someday," she said.

"Yeah." Wes nodded happily, but inside he worried what she would think of his patchwork family and the way they still moved in their own orbits.

They rounded the corner to the four-plex workstation. Their

29

workmates, Ravi Chopra and Jeff Spooner, lit up like glow sticks when they saw Wes.

"Dude, how was Vegas?" Ravi asked.

"Did you count cards?" Jeff asked.

"Did you see the Blue Man Group?"

"Did you see the Hoover Dam?"

Meg shook her head. "Seriously? Guys, Wes was in Vegas solving his dad's case—he didn't have time to be a tourist." She set down her phone and backpack. "I'm going to get coffee."

The guys watched her walk away, then swung back to Wes.

Jeff looked contrite. "Congrats on getting your parents back, Dude."

"Yeah, congrats," Ravi added.

Jeff leaned in. "But tell me you at least had time to see the Pinball Hall of Fame?"

Wes set down his phone and backpack. "And to think I actually missed you two goobers."

They suddenly straightened and pretended to be studying their laptop screens. Wes looked up to see their "boss" Richard McCormick, rolling toward them. The guy was a slouchy geek, but smart and nice enough.

"Hi, Wesley."

"Hello, sir," Wes said, dipping his chin.

"Got a minute to step into my office?"

Wes's pulse blipped. Was he being let go? How would he convince Meg to tell him she loved him again if he wasn't around? "Sure."

"Bring your things."

Jeff and Ravi looked worried for him. Wes retrieved his backpack and phone, then followed McCormick back through the maze of cubicles to his office. Towers of printouts engulfed his desk, and a half dozen computers in various stages of repair sat along a rear table, with tangles of cords underneath.

"I know I have an extra chair here somewhere," McCormick

said, scratching his head. "Ah, here it is."

Obscured by more stacks of paper. He picked up the heap between the armrests and dropped it on the floor where it promptly fell over. "Have a seat," McCormick said.

Wes lowered himself gingerly.

"Dammit," McCormick muttered. "I forgot to pick up the forms I need to go over with you, and they're on the printer one floor up. Sit tight, and I'll be back in a few."

Dismissal forms, no doubt, Wes thought. McCormick had probably figured out he'd left a backdoor for himself when he'd initially hacked into the courthouse database so he could go back in at his leisure and search for transcripts of his father's court case. He'd been periodically doing database dumps hoping to find something helpful, but had come up empty.

And it was all a moot point now, wasn't it?

Still, McCormick would be within his rights to report him, revoke his community service hours, and send him back to jail.

His leg began to jump and he experienced another flash craving for Oxy. Just to take the edge off. He lifted his hand and chewed on a hangnail until it bled. Cursing at the pain, he pulled out his phone to pass the time until McCormick came back to fire him.

But when he spotted the Georgia Tech sticker on the black case, he frowned—this wasn't his phone... it was Meg's. When the urge to snoop rose in his mind, he set it down... for five whole seconds. He tapped the screen, expecting to see a passcode keyboard that would keep him from accessing her private emails and texts, but to his surprise, Meg Vincent didn't have her phone secured.

Which, he reasoned, was practically an invitation to poke around.

He tapped on the messaging icon to scan her texts. Their last conversation was still there, and a message from her mother, one from her friend Lori, and one from someone named Candy.

He stopped at the next name, then frowned. Mark, the preppie dude he'd seen her out with a few times. She'd said he was a friend of her brother who'd died of an overdose, and Wes believed her. But he also believed Mark was trying to get into Meg's pants.

He tapped on the conversation and scanned the texts, surprised to see his name.

Wes gave me a beautiful bracelet

Is that supposed to make up for what he did?

The baby isn't his

But coulda been. He's a loser, Meg

Wes frowned. What a dick.

He's had a tough life

Waah, who hasn't?

You haven't

Wes snickered. Go, Meg.

You deserve better

He messed up, but I think he really cares about me

He wants to screw you

Probably... but so do you

Good, she had the guy pegged.

True, but I'm offering you more than that

"And I'm back," McCormick boomed, startling him. The man was sweating as if he'd run a marathon, and held up the sheets of paper as if they were the prize. "Got 'em." He swung triumphantly into the rolling chair behind his piled up desk.

Wes reluctantly put away Meg's phone. "Look, Dude, if you're kicking me out, just say so."

McCormick's head came up. "Huh? Wes, I'm not kicking you out."

"You're not?"

"No. I'm offering you a job."

Wes's eyebrows climbed. "A job?"

"Yeah." He held up the papers. "This is the offer. It's only at half-rate until you fulfill your community service obligation, but after that, it's not bad pay for a part-time job."

"Part-time?"

"Twenty hours a week," McCormick said. "You'd be supervising the students doing work studies."

His eyebrows climbed higher. "You mean Meg and Ravi and Jeff?"

"Right. I've been keeping an eye on you. The others seem to follow your lead. You're a good coder and you don't even have formal training."

Wes shrugged. "I've been playing with code since I was a kid."

"You're a natural," McCormick said, handing him the papers. "Take these with you and read them over. Talk to your probation officer, and let me know if you have any questions."

He stood and took the papers. "Okay… thanks."

"You're welcome. By the way, really good news about your parents."

Wes nodded. "Thanks, man."

"Now get back to work."

Wes left, but took his time walking back to the work station, scrolling through the rest of Meg's text conversation with Mark.

We've talked about his before

Let's talk about it again… Tom would approve

Don't bring him into this… I gotta go… talk later

Tom must be Meg's brother.

Wes frowned—just as he suspected, Marky Mark the Metrosexual was after his girl.

He exited the messages app, then slipped the phone and the job offer into his backpack. When he rounded the corner to the workstation, he was toying with whether to tell his friends he might be their boss, just to mess with them. But he stopped when he saw Meg was talking on a cell phone—*his* cell phone—and Ravi and Jeff were rapt.

"You don't say," Meg was saying. "Wes did that, did he?"

He frowned. Who could she be talking to? His sister? Mouse?

Meg looked up and noticed him. "Oh, you're in luck, here's

33

Wes now. Uh-huh… good talking to you, too."

She stood and extended the phone to Wes, looking smug. "Our phones got switched."

"Sorry," he mumbled, reaching into his backpack to retrieve hers and exchange. "Who is it?'

"Alexis," she said brightly.

He squinted. "I don't know an Alexis."

"Really? Because she came up on your phone as 'Big Knockers.' "

That wasn't specific enough to ring a bell—he was kind of into boobs.

"She works in Vegas," Meg continued, "says you gave her two counterfeit one hundred dollar bills and she wants her money, pronto."

He closed his eyes briefly. The busty waitress who flirted with him and served him beer. He'd been winning big, so he tipped her big… with phony bills. She'd given him her number, but how had she gotten his? "Uh… I can explain."

Meg gave him a smile that was as fake as the money he'd spent in Vegas. "Alexis is the one you owe an explanation to."

He covered his phone mic. "She was a waitress in the casino," he whispered frantically. "Nothing happened. It couldn't have—I was arrested right after I met her."

"You were arrested at the casino?"

Uh-oh. "Um… yeah."

"So if you hadn't been arrested, something would've happened with Alexis?"

Wes saw the critical error in his defense. "Er…"

Meg dropped something on his phone screen—the rose gold bracelet.

"Maybe that'll cover her losses," she said, then picked up her backpack, and left.

Wes groaned. They were so *not* dating.

CHAPTER 5

"NAME OF INMATE?" the guy on the other side of the window asked.

"Ashford," Carlotta said. "Peter Ashford."

"And your name? Spell it please."

She did.

"Okay, read the text on the screen and if you agree, check the box and sign your name with the digital pen."

An ominous three paragraphs came up, including language that she agreed not to hold the Fulton County Correctional Facility liable for any injuries, physical or mental, that might occur during her visit, up to and including death.

She signed her name, then took a seat in the designated waiting area until visiting time commenced. She nodded at the other visitors waiting to see loved ones, remembering other times when she'd waited to see Wesley and once, Coop, when they had been arrested on various charges. But this somehow felt worse because as concerned as she'd been, she'd known Wes and Coop had the street smarts to cope with incarceration. Peter Ashford, who had been raised with a silver spoon in every orifice, had no such skills.

A guard came in with a clipboard and called off names for everyone to queue up. They were led in a group to a long narrow room with a bank of phones along a Plexiglass wall. She went to her assigned booth and lowered herself into the hard chair. Behind a thick wall of glass, a man was being led to the seat in front of her. She had to look twice to realize it was Peter. Dressed in drab gray pants and shirt, he was unrecognizable. His hands were cuffed in front of him. He kept his head bowed until the guard removed them. When he looked up, his face was pale and gaunt, and his hair was overlong. But he did seem happy to see her.

Carlotta picked up the handset on her side, and he followed suit. "Hi," she said, forcing a smile to her lips.

He smiled and looked more like himself. "Hi, Carly."

"How are you?" they each asked at the same time.

"You first," he said. "Tell me everything you can in fifteen minutes."

She nodded. "I'm fine, just adjusting to having my family back together."

"How's your mother?"

Her smile faltered. "Not well, but we're hoping new doctors will be able to help her."

He wet his lips. "And Randolph?"

"Good... remarkably so. He's almost completely healed from his injuries."

"And your little sister, wow, that had to be a big shock."

She laughed. "It was... but Prissy's been a blessing. She's funny and bright, and she seems resilient. She's our common thread as we try to find our way through all of this."

He nodded, then his eyes suddenly welled with tears. "I'm so sorry, Carly."

"Peter, don't—"

"I have to say this," he cut in. "I'm sorry I pressured you to marry me. I guess in the back of my mind I wanted us to be committed in the event something like this happened."

She blinked. "You mean, so I would be less likely to leave?"

"It was selfish, I know. I just love you so much, I was afraid I'd lose you." His throat convulsed. "And I have."

Her chest welled with emotion. "I told you I would still support you, Peter. You need to focus on your case. When does your attorney think you'll be out of here?"

"Unfortunately, my case is being lumped in with Walt Tully, Ray Mashburn, and Brody Jones, and the D.A. thinks we're all a flight risk."

And after spending the last decade looking for Randolph, he wasn't taking any chances.

"I hear Walt Tully is being monitored like a hawk and as soon as the D.A. is convinced he's well enough to incarcerate, he's going to be locked up in here, too. But my attorney is working hard to separate my case from theirs, and my dad is lobbying on my behalf."

The Ashfords had deep roots in the business and political community. Hopefully his father would be able to pull in some favors.

"If it's any consolation," she said, "Randolph told me he didn't think you were aware of what was going on at Mashburn & Tully until the very end. And he told the D.A. as much. If he thought you were in on framing him, he wouldn't have called you at the office that time to ask for your help."

Peter nodded. "My attorney told me Randolph is willing to testify on my behalf. It's big of him considering what the firm put him through."

"He seems to be in a forgiving mindset." She smiled. "Hannah is championing you, too."

He scoffed. "Calling clients to tell them to withdraw money before everything imploded seemed like the least I could do."

"But by making those calls, you sacrificed your own freedom. That was an honorable thing to do, Peter, and hopefully the D.A. will agree."

The guard in the back of the room cleared his throat. "Two minute warning," he announced to the visitors.

The desolate look in Peter's eyes made her heart race. "Do you need anything?"

He shook his head. "Thank you for coming, Carly. You're my

world, do you know that?"

She managed a smile. "You'll be out of here soon."

He nodded, but she could tell he didn't believe it. He put his hand on the window between them and she reluctantly put her hand over his. A bell rang, signaling an end to visitation.

"Goodbye," she murmured.

When he didn't respond, she returned the handset to its cradle, then stood, waved, and walked away.

As she stood in line to reclaim her personal belongings, Carlotta reflected on Peter's admission that he'd hoped they'd be married before the Mashburn & Tully house of cards tumbled so she'd be more likely to stand by him.

There it was again—the gut-clenching sensation that she'd escaped a close call, but this time by not marrying Peter.

It was enough to make a woman seriously question her own judgment.

She was still collecting herself as she stood near the parking deck and summoned a ride-share car service, wondering if any drivers would respond considering the pickup spot was the county jail. At the sound of footsteps behind her, she stepped aside to allow the pedestrian to pass, then blinked in surprise at the sight of the man who appeared deep in thought. "Jack?"

His head swung up and his face rearranged into something that resembled friendliness. "Carlotta... hi. What are you doing here?"

"Visiting Peter."

"Ah. How is Ashford?"

"As good as can be expected, I suppose." She noticed he was carrying a Macy's bag. "What are you doing here?"

He squirmed, then spoke in the general direction of her knees. "Dropping off some things for Liz."

"Oh."

"She's being held here until the psych evaluations are completed." He held up the bag. "It's basic stuff, pajamas and... underwear. I thought it might... help."

"That's nice of you," she murmured, newly awash in how awkward and sad the entire Liz situation was for everyone concerned. *If only...*

He gave a curt nod, then lifted a strained smile. "Tell Prissy I said hi."

"I will." She noticed the driver of a car service looking for a passenger and lifted her hand. "Here's my taxi. Bye."

The car pulled up next to the curb. Jack opened the door for her, and she slid inside.

"You know you can call me if you ever... need anything." His expression was tormented.

"I know, Jack."

He closed the door.

As the car pulled away, Carlotta looked back to see him turning toward the jail. Her heart was tied in a knot.

CHAPTER 6

WES SAT STRAIGHT up in bed from a dead sleep. A loud banging noise sounded from the living room.

"What the hell?" he muttered, feeling for his glasses on the nightstand. A half-dozen scenarios went through his head about what bad guy could have broken into the townhome this time. One of Hollis Carver's guys, one of Dillon Carver's guys, someone he'd beat in a card game, someone looking for his buddy Chance...

Wincing against the daylight streaming through the window, he rolled out of bed. After grabbing the golf club leaning against the wall, he yanked open his bedroom door and stumbled into the hall, raising the club as he ran into the living room.

His dad paused from hammering a nail into a bare stud and grinned. "Good morning."

Wes's shoulders dropped in relief. "Dad... what are you doing here?"

"I thought we were going to get started on the repairs today."

Wes dragged his hand down his face. "I meant what are you doing here so early?"

Randolph laughed. "Early? It's eight-thirty, son."

Wes stood, blinking. "I was up late..." Playing video poker. "Um, sanding drywall mud." He gestured toward a small patched section.

Randolph glanced around at the gaping holes in the walls. "Dillon's guys really did a number on this place."

"Yeah," Wes said. "I'm sure Liz told them to leave no stone unturned. It's a good thing you stashed only some of the counterfeit bills here." He pointed to an area next to the door. "That's where I found it."

Randolph nodded. "I remember when I put it there." He made a rueful noise. "I thought I'd be back soon to get it and turn all of the counterfeit loot over to the FBI. Things just went sideways… and time kept sliding." Then he seemed to shake himself. "But enough about that. Hey, nice driver."

He set down the hammer and took the club Wes was holding. It was the club Mouse had bought for him.

"Glad to see you've been playing," Randolph said, adopting a driving stance and pantomiming a slow motion swing.

He wondered what his dad would think if he told him he'd used it as a weapon to threaten The Carver's delinquent clients.

His dad smiled and handed it back. "I'll get us a tee time at the club."

"Sure," Wes said. Everyone kept saying how much he resembled Randolph, but the man standing before him might as well have been an alien. He was handsome and lean, ruggedly tanned, yet groomed like a catalog model. Even his work clothes were Abercrombie cool and rumpled just the right amount. Wes couldn't pull that off if he tried.

Randolph pointed toward the kitchen. "I put on some coffee, picked up some bagels."

Wes stared at his dad just standing there in the living room, still expecting to wake up from a dream to find he'd imagined the events of the last few weeks and his parents were still missing.

"Wes?"

He blinked. "Huh?"

"Are you okay?"

"Yeah. Just not fully awake yet."

"Go wash up and let's have breakfast."

Let's have breakfast. As if they'd been having breakfast

together for the past ten years.

His dad had so easily resumed his place in life, and Carlotta seemed to be taking things in stride, too. Prissy acted as if she'd always been around. Obviously he was the only one struggling with the new Wren family dynamic.

"Okay. Give me a few minutes to feed Einstein."

"Einstein?"

"My python."

Randolph's eyes widened. "You have a snake?"

"Yeah. He's cool. Do you want to see him?"

Randolph shook his head. "No thanks. Besides, that's more of a boy's pet, don't you think?"

That smarted. "I... guess so."

Randolph gave a dismissive wave. "We can talk about that later. How do you like your coffee?"

He liked adding copious amounts of cream and sugar, but suddenly that seemed juvenile, too. "Black... the stronger, the better."

"Good," Randolph said with ringing approval, then walked toward the kitchen.

Wes felt an anxiety headache descend like a bucket of thick paint being poured over his head. The urge for a hit of Oxy hit him hard, teased him, then moved on. He exhaled slowly, then retraced his steps to his bedroom. Einstein was basking in a warm light in his aquarium.

"Hi, boy," Wes said, tapping lightly on the glass.

The black and grey spotted axanthic ball python turned its head toward the vibration and sent its ribbon tongue slithering out.

"Are you hungry? You haven't eaten in a while."

He reached for the shoebox on his bookshelf and lifted the lid. Inside, a little white mouse ran for its life around the perimeter of the box. Wes nabbed it with tongs, then unlocked a little opening in the aquarium lid.

"Sorry, little buddy... but you know the drill."

The mouse did, having participated in this torturous exercise the previous day. It hit the bottom of the aquarium running, searching frantically for cover from the python. But if Einstein was tempted by the scurrying snack this time, he didn't let on.

"I'll let you think about it for a while," Wes said, then relocked the opening. His father's comment about snakes being for boys came back to him.

Maybe it was time to find Einstein a new home. He'd gotten him as a baby from an adoption and rescue society. At the time they'd told him they would take him back someday if necessary. Many pet owners set them free, but the wilds of Atlanta, Georgia was not a python-friendly environment.

Wes tabled the decision, then washed his face, scrubbed his teeth, and jumped into ratty jeans, T-shirt, and old tennis shoes. He checked on Einstein and the mouse again—still status quo— then left his room and headed toward the kitchen.

He was amped up about spending the day with Randolph, he told himself... so why were his feet so heavy?

Randolph was standing in the kitchen doorway, but staring at the sad little metallic Christmas tree sitting among the debris just inside the living room.

"Is that what I think it is?" he asked.

"It's the tree that was up when you and Mom... left."

Randolph squatted and pulled a dusty gift-wrapped box from beneath a chunk of drywall. "You and Carlotta didn't open the gifts?"

Wes shook his head. "We decided to wait until we were all together again."

Randolph put his hand over his mouth. Wes could tell he was holding back tears, which sent a lump to his own throat.

"We'll wait until your mother is having a good day."

Wes nodded, trying to hold it together.

Randolph cleared his throat. "Let's eat."

The kitchen was in bad shape, too, holes everywhere. In fact, every surface in every room of the townhome would have to be repaired and painted.

Wes opened the box of bagels, then retrieved a knife for the cream cheese.

As Randolph poured coffee into two mugs, he studied the spot where he'd planted a listening device in the wall to eavesdrop on snatches of Wes and Carlotta's lives through a receiver on the few occasions he'd come back to Atlanta while living as a fugitive. "Did Dillon's thugs find the bug?"

"No," Wes said. "One of The Carver's guys. But he's a friend, was helping me install a burglar alarm."

"A friend?" Randolph carried the coffee to the table. "How is it you're friends with someone who works for a brute like Hollis Carver?"

"Uh... it's a long story."

"I've got time," his dad said, taking a seat.

Wes sat, too, wondering how much of his illicit activities to divulge. He bought time smearing a sesame seed bagel with cream cheese. "I owed money to The Carver and to another guy named Father Thom."

"Why?"

"Poker," he said.

Disapproval darkened his father's face. "You must not be very good at it."

Wes bit down on the inside of his cheek. "I'm better now. I was killing it in Vegas."

"How much?"

"I was gambling with twenty-five, only used half that and won another twenty-five." He frowned. "Until it was all confiscated."

"How'd you get so good?"

Wes shrugged. "Lots of video poker. And a good memory."

Randolph pursed his mouth. "Got a deck handy?"

Wes went over to a drawer, opened it and pulled out a deck of cards. "Will these do?"

Randolph reached for them, then opened the box and began to shuffle like a pro. "Sit down," he said with a nod.

Wes sat. "How long were you a dealer?"

"A while. Mostly blackjack, but a little poker. Take a look at these cards."

He dealt twenty cards face up on the table in quick succession, then he scooped them up and turned them over. He held and fanned the undealt cards so only he could see. "What do I have left?"

"All the Jacks," Wes said. "Everything else is mostly fives or lower. One ace, one queen."

Randolph glanced over the cards and nodded. "Not bad."

Wes savored his dad's praise.

"So you were saying you owed money to both of these loan sharks," he prompted.

"Yeah. The Carver bought my debt from Father Thom, and in order to pay him back, I started riding along with one of his guys, Mouse, to help with collections."

His father's jaw hardened. "Owing money to a loan shark is one thing... but working for one—that's unacceptable."

Randolph's censure cut deep. Wes took a bite of the bagel and chewed, studying the design on the deli box.

"Do you still owe him money?"

Wes swallowed. "I, uh... settled my debt with some of the money I found in the wall before I went to Vegas." When his father looked alarmed, he quickly added, "But that turned out to be a good thing because when The Carver saw it, he thought Dillon was back in the money laundering business. Dillon told my buddy Chance that me paying with fake bills had gotten him into a lot of trouble with his dad, and that's how Carlotta and I pieced together what was going on."

Randolph nodded thoughtfully. "Luckily, it all worked out. How much do you still owe?"

Wes coughed, then told him. Randolph lifted an eyebrow, then pulled out his wallet and counted out the amount in crisp hundreds. "And these aren't fake," he added with a little smile.

Wes stared at the brick of money. "I can't take that."

"Why not?"

"Because it's my debt, not yours."

"Which you wouldn't have incurred if I'd been around to keep you from making that mistake, among others."

That mistake and others. So his father did see him as a failure. He kept chewing.

"Like this body moving business you got your sister involved in," Randolph said.

Wes swallowed the mush in his mouth. "It was the only job I could get at the time. And my driver's license is suspended, so Carlotta drove me to a couple of jobs and got herself involved." He frowned. "If you haven't noticed, she has a mind of her own. Plus Coop has a thing for Carlotta, so he didn't exactly dissuade her."

"The doctor has a thing for her? I thought that detective had a thing for her."

Wes rolled his eyes. "They both do."

"But she was engaged to Peter."

"I think Carlotta just finally gave in to Peter," Wes said. "Besides, the engagement only lasted ten minutes."

"So who do you think will win out?"

"Jack's out of the running."

"How so?"

"You don't know? He's the father of Liz's baby."

Randolph took a drink of coffee from his mug. "No, I hadn't heard."

Wes took his time chewing a bite, studying his father's averted face. "Have you talked to Liz?"

"No. Why would I?"

So he was going to play it that way. "Because she was your... lawyer."

Randolph scoffed. "She set me up."

Wes took a drink of coffee, fighting not to wince at the bitter taste. Liz had made a lot of mistakes, and he hated her for threatening his mother and sisters, but a part of him admired that she'd been so desperate to make sure her baby had a good life that it had driven her to the edge of reason.

"Liz was my, um… lawyer, too, you know."

His dad stopped mid-chew.

Wes could see he was wrestling with incredulity that a hot mature woman like Liz would want to sleep with a skinny nineteen-year-old.

"I hope she… *represented* you better than she represented me," Randolph said lightly.

"I have no complaints," Wes said, matching his tone.

His dad took another drink of coffee, presumably to wash down the revelation. "I guess you've grown up in more ways than one while I was away."

"Guess so," Wes agreed.

"I saw the motorcycle in the garage—I assume it's yours."

"Yeah. I bought it from a pawn shop." The lady there had been nice enough to take back the engagement ring he'd bought for Liz in trade for the crotch rocket. "Until my license is reinstated, though, I'm stuck riding my ten-speed."

"As soon as your license is reinstated, we'll get you a car," his dad said casually.

Wes's pulse blipped. "A Mustang?"

"I was thinking more like a Beamer," Randolph said. "Image is important."

Wes's enthusiasm dimmed a bit… but a car was a car.

"I see Carlotta still has her Miata."

Wes nodded. "It hasn't run in years. She got stuck with a car she took for a test drive on a lark, but it got blown up. Then she drove one of Peter's cars and managed to smash it up. She's been driving a rental for a while."

"So maybe two Beamers," Randolph said with a smile.

Wes glanced at the pile of cash in front of him. "Are we rich again?"

His dad laughed. "Between dealing at the casinos and day trading, yeah—I did alright. And now that I'm back—" He nodded to the cash. "—there's a lot more where that came from."

Wes grinned. He could get used to being the kid of a rich man.

"What about you, son? What are you planning to do with your life?"

His grin dissolved. "I… haven't really thought about it."

"Well, you'd better be thinking about it. By the time I was your age, I was already interning at a Big 8 accounting firm."

"I have options," Wes murmured. "My boss at my community service job for the city offered me a part-time job."

Randolph made a face. "A government job? My son can do better than that."

Wes chewed on his tongue. He could?

"If my situation has taught you anything, it's that money makes the world go around."

Wes nodded. How well he knew, from the position of never having any.

"You have to get out there and make things happen, get your hands dirty. You can't do that sitting in a cubicle in some stuffy city building."

Wes kept nodding. But there was Meg…

Then Randolph looked around at the disarray and sighed. "Speaking of getting our hands dirty, we'd better get started." He stood, then picked up the stack of cash on the table and pressed it into Wes's hand. "Get square with The Carver. I don't want him to have any power over you."

His dad walked to the coffee pot for a refill.

Wes stared at the money, then back to his father. But would this mean Randolph would now have power over him?

CHAPTER 7

"LADIES AND GENTLEMEN," the male announcer boomed in an undulating voice worthy of a professional sportscast, "are you ready for Rooooooooller Derby?"

Carlotta cheered, but her voice was lost in the roar of the crowd gathered in the gymnasium to watch the match. Music with a heart-jarring bass blasted from overhead speakers, while swirling strobe lights made it feel as if the entire facility was spinning.

"This is so cool!" Prissy shouted.

Carlotta was happy to see her sister happy. Wes and Chance were on the other side of Priscilla, adding their yells and fist pumps. Wes was happy, too, she observed with a pang. Everywhere she looked, everyone was happy, happy, happy.

So what was her problem?

"Is this seat taken?" Coop shouted near her ear.

She turned and grinned, conceding that this man's presence made her as close to happy as she'd been lately. Coop was tall and fit and effortlessly cool in jeans and a pale blue shirt, untucked. Behind dark-rimmed glasses were intelligent eyes that had seen their share of problems, but he was eternally optimistic. She made room for him on the bleacher.

"I thought you'd changed your mind," she said behind a cupped hand to be heard over the melee.

"Sorry—busy day at work."

Coop had stepped in when the Chief Medical Examiner had

been arrested, and although he'd said a replacement was imminent, for the meantime, he seemed to be working long hours.

"Hi, Dr. Coop!" Prissy yelled. He reached around Carlotta to tug Prissy's pigtail, then waved hello to Wes.

"Will you be dancing tonight?" Prissy asked.

Coop looked confused.

"She overheard me and Hannah talking about *body moving* and I had to improvise," Carlotta said for his ears only.

"Ah." He grinned, then leaned forward. "No dancing, but I was thinking about getting ice cream afterward. Wanna come?"

Prissy grinned and nodded enthusiastically.

He looked at Carlotta and winced. "Hope that's okay?"

Carlotta smiled. "Only if I'm invited too."

"We'll make room, won't we Prissy?"

"If we have to," Prissy said—and she wasn't joking.

Carlotta looked back to Coop and shook her head.

He smothered a laugh. "Wow, look at this crowd. I had no idea the sport was so popular."

"Same here," Carlotta said.

"How did Hannah get into roller derby?"

"She said someone came up to her in a bar and said she looked like someone who would be in roller derby. She was intrigued, and found out the local league was putting on a camp for beginners, so she signed up. And apparently the team she's playing for is short a blocker, so they asked if she would step in."

When the noise ratcheted back a few decibels he asked, "So what did I miss?"

"The announcer and the mascots did a mini demonstration for the newbies. I'll tell you what I remember. This is flat track derby, so the oval taped off on the floor shows the inbounds and out of bounds areas, and where the skaters line up."

"How many on each team?"

"Five on the floor at once. Oh, wait—unless skaters are in the penalty box."

"For?"

"I remember Hannah saying they're not allowed to throw elbows or punch or trip anyone."

Coop scoffed. "You mean I'm not going to see any girl fights tonight?"

She laughed. "Maybe you'll get lucky."

He turned his head and locked gazes with her. "Now I'm thinking about something else entirely."

Her lips parted slightly. Dammit, now she was, too.

Coop cleared his throat and tore his gaze from hers. "How long is a match?"

She looked back to the track. "Two thirty-minute periods, but they're broken down into shorter scoring sessions called jams."

"Jams... okay. How does the scoring work?"

"Each team has a head skater called the jammer—she's the one with the star on her helmet. When the whistle blows, the jammer from each team tries to break through the blockers. Whichever one makes it through first is the lead jammer. The jammers score points for every skater on the other team they lap."

"So like Red Rover, Red Rover?"

Carlotta thought about the childhood game where teammates locked hands and someone from the opposing team ran and tried to break through. "Yeah, kind of. I guess we'll understand more when the match starts."

Coop craned his neck. "Where's Hannah?"

"She was skating earlier to warm up, but her team went into their locker room. Wait—here they come now!"

"Rooooller Derby fans," the announcer said, "put your hands together for the Bruised Peaches!"

The crowd went wild as the female team of about a dozen skaters zoomed onto the floor and huddled, chanting and pumping each other up. The announcer made a big deal of introducing each member of the team by their campy "stage" name, like Evil Sheila, Brenda Blender, and Missy Behavin'. The skaters wore unitards in the teams colors of black and peach, but customized their outfit, helmet, and skates with numbers and patches like POW! and GET BACK! They all wore elbow and knee pads, and wrist guards. Each woman was glammed up to varying degrees with makeup and hair reminiscent of the pin-up era. And each had their own cheering section with posters and fans who showed their support with wild outfits and noisemakers.

"Hannah's next!" Prissy shouted, jumping up and down.

Carlotta pulled out her phone to capture her friend on video.

"New phone?" Coop asked.

"Uh-huh. I'm still getting used to it."

"That's okay. Change is good," he murmured in a way that made her think he wasn't talking about smart phones.

"Making her derby debut this evening," the announcer shouted, "is number sixty-nine, Hannah the Hammer!"

Carlotta laughed at Hannah's number and name choice. Hannah skated her solo turn around the track with style, flexing her biceps and hamming it up for the spectators as she sped by. She was statuesque and gorgeous with dark red lips, dramatic blue eye shadow, and colorful tattoos.

Carlotta and the gang all cheered and waved, Chance the loudest.

"Go, Babe! Go, Hannah!" Then he turned to the crowd behind them and happily shouted, "That's my wife!"

"How'd that happen?" some guy yelled, referring to Chance's general averageness, and everyone laughed.

"I have money," Chance yelled back good-naturedly, garnering more laughs.

Carlotta agreed Wes's chubby buddy and hardbody Hannah were an unlikely match. Their relationship was unorthodox—Chance didn't know Hannah was heir to the HAL Properties fortune, which likely surpassed Chance's trust fund. And there was the not-living-together thing. But they seemed to be equally enamored with each other.

And who was she to judge? It wasn't as if she'd mastered the art of romance.

Coop reached over and absently patted her knee with affection.

She glanced up at his winsome profile. *Yet.*

Despite the rough and tumble reputation of roller derby, Carlotta was surprised to see the event was actually a family affair, with lots of kids Prissy's age and younger in attendance, many of them there to cheer on a skating sister, aunt, mother or even grandmother. Hannah had mentioned the derby was like one big community, and that was evident tonight.

After the last skater for the Bruised Peaches was introduced, the music reset to a menacing beat.

"And now," the announcer said, his voice low and dramatic, "welcome to the floor last year's league champions, the Traffic Stoppers!"

The opposing team burst onto the track like a swarm of angry bees. If the Bruised Peaches evoked a flirtatious retro vibe, the Traffic Stoppers were going for the biker girl image. Their uniforms and gear had an industrial, grungy look, and their body language and stage names were tough: Blood Letty, Destroyer LaToya, and Wreck-it Wendy. They made faces at the crowd and growled at the other team when they skated by. But it was all in good fun, and the crowd loved the setup of the two teams' rivalry.

Mascots from both teams entertained the crowd while the skaters prepared to take the floor. Representing the Bruised Peaches was a big, strong looking guy wearing a comically unflattering beige unitard, a green wig and sporting two black eyes that were obviously some kind of makeup. He ran around the perimeter of the track, leading cheers and generally getting the crowd on its feet. His full-out enthusiasm was contagious. Carlotta recorded his antics on video, as well as the opposing team's mascot, also a man, who wore an over-the-top leather vest, shorts, and boots ensemble, with red bandanna and a cape. The two mascots competed in mock races around the track and tossed

T-shirts into the stands. She wondered if their girlfriends or wives were derby girls.

"Please help me in thanking the teams' sponsors," the announcer said. "Tannenbaum's All Natural Energy Drink—shake it up, and it'll shake you up. And Riggles Chiropractic Center, where they bend over backward to make you feel better."

The crowd laughed and groaned at the pun.

"Seriously, folks, please give these businesses your patronage, and if you have a product or service you'd like to get in front of our enthusiastic followers, remember that roller derby is a largely volunteer organization, so we're always looking for more sponsors."

"I'll speak to my uncle about the funeral home sponsoring some matches," Coop said. "It's hard to find an affordable family sporting event to sponsor." He gave her a crooked smile. "And this crowd doesn't seem like it would be put off by death."

The Bruised Peaches mascot was in front of their section shimmying to the music, and bellowing like a wild man.

"It's an interesting cast of characters, for sure," she agreed. "That guy might've had too much of the energy drink."

The lights came up and the officials skated onto the floor. The fans' fervor increased as the skaters lined up, four blockers from each team, with the two jammers on the other side of the line, facing the pack. Carlotta could see why the peaches had wanted Hannah as a blocker. The derby girls were all shapes and sizes, but Hannah was the tallest woman on the floor. Still, the blockers from the other team didn't seem intimidated as they positioned themselves with toe brakes, shoulders down, heads up.

A whistle blew, and the match began. The jammers lunged forward, using their shoulders and hips to try to break through the pack. The blockers jockeyed to prevent the opposing jammer from getting through, while trying to create an opening for their own jammer. For Hannah and the other blockers, it was a controlled dance of skating backwards and sideways.

Suddenly, the Bruised Peaches jammer saw an opening and skated past the pack, straining, but managing to stay inbounds. An official pointed to her, designating her as lead jammer. She sped up and skated by herself around the track to deafening cheers. When she approached the pack again, she put down her shoulders and prepared to battle for points. Once again the wall of blockers tried to stop her from passing. She leaned in, then suddenly pivoted to the side and passed the pack, racking up five points for lapping the four blockers, and the other team's jammer, who was still trapped, thanks to the Peaches' blockers. In the points celebration, though, the Traffic Stoppers' jammer broke away, pumping like crazy to build speed. Then the jammer for the Peaches brought her hands to her hips in a chopping motion. Whistles sounded and the referees all repeated the jammer's hands-to-hips motion, then the skaters relaxed and skated out of position.

"What just happened?" Coop asked.

"The jam can last for two minutes," Carlotta said, "but the lead jammer can call it off early to keep the other jammer from lapping around and scoring. That's the hand signal to call it off."

"Ah, okay… I think I'm catching on."

"I'm still learning, too," Carlotta said with a laugh. "But this is fun."

The announcer updated the score and the skaters reassembled in front and behind the designated lines to kick off another jam. This time the Traffic Stoppers' jammer got a break, lapped around, and scored four points. Each jam threw the momentum to the alternate team so that by the last jam before the end of the half, they were neck and neck at eighty and eight-two points, with the Bruised Peaches leading. Various penalties had been called for illegal contact and other rules infractions, resulting in players being banished to the penalty box for times ranging from thirty seconds to a minute or two.

As the skaters assumed their positions for the final jam of the period, there seemed to be some smack talk going back and forth, and Hannah was right in the middle of it, standing toe to toe with a Traffic Stopper blocker who outweighed her by fifty pounds. When the whistle sounded, suddenly Hannah's head popped back, and blood appeared on her chin. More whistles sounded and before she could land the punch she'd wound up, a referee placed herself between Hannah and the opposing blocker. The official blew the whistle again, gesturing to the other player and tapping her own helmet.

"A head blocking penalty has been the called against the star blocker of the Traffic Stoppers," the announcer said. The player skated off the track to the penalty box to jeers from Bruised Peaches fans.

"Boo on you!" Chance shouted, pointing with exaggeration. "Boo on you!" The crowd behind them took up the chant, then the Peaches mascot took over and fanned the flame. Time out was called to bandage Hannah's chin. Throughout she glared at the player who'd hit her and the woman glared back.

"You might get that fight after all," Carlotta said to Coop.

Before coming to the event tonight, she had passed off roller derby as a fake sport, like men's professional wrestling—more performance than competition. Especially since there was a cosplay element to the culture that extended to the spectators and vendors. But watching the skaters in full equipment jockey for position, it was clear there was nothing fake about the athleticism on display. These women were fierce.

The mascots rushed onto the floor to entertain during the timeout. Carlotta kept recording Hannah because she knew her friend would want to see the injury and the aftermath. Once the bandage was in place, Hannah skated back onto the track to the tune of loud cheers, and waved to the crowd.

"She's in her element," Coop said.

Carlotta agreed. The layers had been peeling off Hannah lately. First Carlotta had discovered her friend was leading a double life as a well-bred Buckhead blueblood, then Hannah admitted she'd initiated a friendship with Carlotta years ago because her family had been victims of Randolph's and she'd been fixated on his daughter. Then the surprise marriage to Chance Hollander in Vegas... and now she was a roller derby queen.

The skaters took their positions again, and the whistle sounded to start the jam.

But over the buzz of anticipation, the Bruised Peaches mascot's voice rang out. "Boo on you!" he was screaming at the blocker sitting a few feet away in the penalty box. *"Boo on you!"*

His behavior seemed overly-aggressive for a family-friendly sport, but when he walked away, Carlotta chalked it up to being caught up in the competition.

Meanwhile, the Peaches were holding the Traffic Stopper's jammer virtually in place, with Hannah shouting encouragement to her team. When the jammer for the Peaches broke free, the fans erupted.

Carlotta was recording it all, but paused when she felt a tug on her sleeve from Prissy. "What?" she asked.

Prissy pointed to the opposite side of the track. "Is the peach man okay?"

The mascot for the Bruised Peaches was sitting on the floor, his back against a column, his feet sprawled in front of him. But his eyes were closed and his head lolled to the side—and gray was not a good color for a peach.

"Coop," Carlotta said, grabbing his arm. "The mascot— something's wrong."

Coop shot to his feet. "Call 911." He pushed his way down the bleachers. "Excuse me, medical emergency, pardon me."

Carlotta punched in the numbers. "Stay here with Wes," she told Prissy, then she followed. When the operator answered, she requested an ambulance to the facility, and described the man as best she could, adding that a doctor was in attendance. Coop had bounded across the track before the skaters had reached that section, but Carlotta found herself dodging skaters, who were dodging her. She tripped and fell on the floor, felt the whoosh of skates barely missing her fingers. Chaos ensued. Referee whistles chorused. Suddenly Hannah was next to her, helping her up. "Carlotta, what the hell?"

"Your mascot is down." She broke free and darted between more skaters to finally clear the track, then sank to her knees next to Coop. He was giving the man chest compressions, his expression grim.

"An ambulance is on the way," she said.

By now everyone realized something had happened to the mascot. A hush had fallen over the gymnasium. The announcer asked everyone to remain quiet. The crowd was standing, necks craned. The skaters dropped to one knee. In the distance the sound of sirens came closer, and ushers hurried to open doors to admit running paramedics. They took over for Coop, checking for a pulse and administering electric shock via paddles. But Carlotta could tell from their reaction they weren't getting a response. After the third shock, they looked up at Coop and shook their heads.

Audible gasps sounded from the audience. Coop walked over to where the officials and the coaches had gathered to break the news. Everyone appeared visibly shaken. The coaches walked away to deliver the news to their teams. There were exclamations of grief and some skaters hugged. A few minutes later, the announcer returned to the microphone.

"Ladies and gentlemen, unfortunately, tonight's match has been cancelled due to a medical emergency." His heavy voice said everything he couldn't put into words. "Please gather your things and head to the nearest exit as quickly as you can. As always, the league appreciates your support and we wish you safe travels home."

Hannah rolled over to Carlotta. "Jesus God, Lewis fucking cheered himself to death?"

Leave it to Hannah to cut to the chase. "What was his name?"

"Lewis Bunning. He was only thirty-two."

She winced. "Did he have family?"

"No. Roller derby was his family."

"I'm sorry for you and your friends."

"Thanks. The girls are taking it hard. Lewis has been with the Peaches since the team was formed, more than five years ago. What can we do?"

Carlotta glanced toward the man's big body, spilling out from under the cloth the paramedics had draped over him. The green wig was also visible. "It would be terrible if pictures got out." She nodded to the fans, craning for a look as they filed by.

Hannah signaled the team to come over. They joined hands to surround the body, many openly crying. Members of the opposing team came over to offer words and hugs of support.

Carlotta looked up into the stands to see Wes shepherding Prissy toward the door, shielding her face with his hands.

"Hey."

She turned to see Coop walking up. "Is there anything I can do to help?" she asked.

He shook his head. "Take Prissy home. God, I hate that she had to see this, and for all the other kids here, too."

"It's so tragic," Carlotta agreed. "Do you think he had a heart attack?"

"Seems likely."

"He looks so young."

"I know, but it happens."

"Are you staying?"

"Yeah. I called the morgue. Someone's bringing a van." He gave her a sad smile. "Raincheck on the ice cream?"

She nodded. "Sure."

"Tell Prissy I'm sorry."

"She'll understand."

"And her sister?"

Carlotta smiled. "She understands, too."

He gave her a grateful nod and a regretful wave. Carlotta turned and joined the queue of tense-faced people heading toward the exits, then pulled out her phone to text Wes she was on her way out.

This made twice Prissy had been with her and a man had died right in front of their eyes—Leonard walking in front of the bus in Vegas, and now at an event that was supposed to be entertaining.

Minus twenty.

CHAPTER 8

"BUCKLE UP," Carlotta told Prissy.

"But the seatbelt will wrinkle my dress," Prissy whined from the backseat.

Carlotta counted to three for patience. Helping Little Miss Clotheshorse get ready for school had been a trying experience, even for someone who'd spent her life dressing people.

"Don't you think it's more important that you arrive safely on your first day of school?"

Prissy screwed up her mouth, thinking it over.

"That was a rhetorical question. Put on your seatbelt, please."

"What's 'rhetorical' mean?"

"It means it makes so much sense, it doesn't require an answer."

Prissy frowned, but pulled out the seatbelt and clicked it into place.

"Thank you."

"You're welcome," Prissy mumbled.

"I'll miss you today."

"I won't miss you."

Push… pull… push. Carlotta's heart went out to her little sister, though. She was being thrust into a new situation and her parents weren't there to ease the way. Randolph had left early again for reasons unknown, and Valerie was having an especially bad day, so Birch was tending to her. Carlotta was frustrated with

Randolph because he seemed to be operating on his own, outside of his family who needed him.

Behavior that was starting to bring back memories of how often he'd worked late when they were growing up and how little he'd known about what was going on in her and Wesley's lives. He had been indulgent, yes... but she realized now it was his way to make up for the time he didn't spend with them.

"You're going to love your new school," Carlotta said with forced optimism.

"I'll be the judge of that," her sister said primly.

Having been put in her place, Carlotta hit the button to raise the garage door and started the engine of the newly purchased sport utility vehicle she shared with Birch. At some point, she had to figure out a more permanent transportation arrangement. Hopefully the new job duties Lindy had promised her before she'd left for Vegas would come with a raise. Randolph was footing the bill for the repairs on the townhome, so with those expenses covered, she might be able to buy a decent vehicle.

When the garage door opened, Prissy lunged forward in her seat. "Jack!"

Standing at the end of the driveway, leaning against his car.

"I see him." Carlotta bit back a curse—she was never going to be able to get over this man if their paths kept crossing.

She pulled the SUV to the end of the driveway, lowered her window and gave Jack a flat smile. "Good morning." Although from his haggard appearance, he hadn't yet been to bed.

Off came Prissy's seatbelt. "Hi, Jack!" she said, sticking her head up next to Carlotta's.

"Hi, Short Stuff. That's a pretty dress."

"Thank you," she sang. "I'm starting school today."

"Lucky you. Are you excited?"

"Yes! I'm going to tell everyone I saw a man *croak* last night."

Carlotta made a rueful noise. "'Croak' isn't a very nice

word."

"It's the word Wesley used. Chance, too. And Hannah."

"My point exactly," Carlotta muttered.

"What's this all about?" Jack asked.

"We went to watch Hannah skate in a roller derby match last night," Carlotta explained, "and a man on the sidelines, um, collapsed."

"And croaked," Prissy added.

He nodded. "I did hear something about that."

"Dr. Coop tried to save him," Prissy offered, "but he croaked anyway."

"Oh, Coop was there."

Carlotta decided it was a rhetorical question.

"Yeah, he sat with us," Prissy answered for her. "He was supposed to take us out for ice cream after, but he couldn't because that man croaked."

Jack wiped his hand over his mouth to conceal a smile.

"Why don't you say 'passed away' instead?" Carlotta suggested. "Or better yet, don't say anything at all. It's not very respectful. Remember, the man's friends and family are very sad he's gone."

"But he died happy," Prissy said. "He was dancing and making people laugh. That's better than the guy in Vegas who got run over by a bus. Isn't it, Jack?"

He seemed taken back. "Um, yeah… if a person has to die, dying happy is definitely the way to go."

Leave it to a child to distill life down to its simplest elements.

Carlotta turned to look at Prissy. "Sit back and put on your seatbelt, please."

Prissy huffed. "You're not my mother!"

Unbidden tears sprang to Carlotta's eyes. The stress of being in the Buckhead house was wearing on her. Horrified, she averted her gaze from Jack's.

"You're right, Prissy," Jack said, his voice gentle. "Carlotta isn't your mother, but she's the next best thing, and she wants you to be safe. Besides, it's the law."

"I know," Prissy said miserably, sitting back to comply. "But it's not good for fashion."

He laughed. "You two definitely fell from the same tree."

"What does that mean?" Prissy asked.

"Never mind," Carlotta said, then pointed to the road. "We should go, Jack. Is everything okay?"

He glanced back to the yard, which was free of photographers. "Uh, yeah. I was just in the neighborhood and I..." He trailed off, and when he looked back to Carlotta, she was struck by the lost look in his eyes. "I guess I just wanted to make sure you're okay."

She smiled, touched and a little bemused as to why he'd be so concerned when, at least to anyone on the outside looking in, everything in her life was finally on the right track. "I'm fine, Jack. Don't worry about me. You have other matters and people to tend to."

"Right. It's just that..." He put both hands on the driver side door. "There are things... I didn't tell you... when I should have."

Her chest suddenly felt tight. She wanted to ask what... but did she really want to know? What would she do if Jack professed his undying love for her? What *could* she do? He was having a baby with another woman, who happened to be in jail for doing some pretty terrible things to her family. It was more than unfair to be teasing her now with *what ifs* and *if onlys*.

Carlotta wet her lips. "Goodbye, Jack."

He nodded and stepped back. "Bye, Prissy. Have a good day at school. Don't break too many hearts."

Prissy was still waving when they pulled out of the driveway. Carlotta tried to put the disconcerting exchange out of her mind and chatted with Prissy to keep her distracted and upbeat. At the school entrance, Carlotta merged into the drop-off lane. In the rear view mirror, she could see the tension on Prissy's face as she watched the girls in the car in front of them emerge and move toward the school entrance, heads together and laughing.

"You'll make a lot of friends," Carlotta said. "You'll see."

Prissy removed her seat belt. "Don't get out." Then she opened the door and jumped out before Carlotta could say anything.

By the time she zoomed down the window, Prissy was already several yards away and climbing the steps to the enormous front doors, her back straight and chin high. Too late, Carlotta realized she'd forgotten to take a picture of Prissy in her first-day dress. She picked up her phone, ready to wave and snap a photo in case her sister looked back.

But she didn't.

A horn sounded behind her. Carlotta sighed, then pulled forward to merge with the long line of cars waiting to exit. The traffic in school zones around Atlanta rivaled the tangle on I-285. She sat and drummed her hand on the steering wheel, trying not to think about Jack's early morning visit and almost-revelation.

Because honestly, who knew what he'd been about to say? It might've had nothing to do with his feelings for her...

But what if it did?

She groaned and willed the cars in front of her to move. To kill time, she pulled up photos from the roller derby to send to Hannah. She ticked through them, discarding duplicates and blurry shots. Then she pulled up some of the videos she'd taken. She smiled when she replayed Hannah's entrance and some of her more theatrical power moves on the track. Coop was right—her friend was in her element.

When she got to the video of Hannah being head-butted by a blocker on the rival team, she winced to see it again. But Hannah would totally love it.

At the corner of the screen, she saw a flash of green, then realized she'd caught the ill-fated mascot on video, pointing and shouting angrily at the player in the penalty box. She remembered thinking his behavior was out of line. As the video rolled, the player yelled something back. They exchanged rude hand gestures and the mascot walked away. He pulled a bottle out of a waist pack and took a drink, then tossed it in a trash can. He went to lean against a column, his body language still agitated. A few seconds later, he slid down the column and his head sagged. It was painful to watch the seconds tick by until she heard her own voice say, "What?" and the video ended—when Prissy had tugged on her sleeve to get her attention.

Carlotta's pulse bumped higher as she rewound the video. She watched it again, this time enlarged so she could focus on Lewis Bunning. He was supremely angry when he confronted the player in the penalty box—the red face and the bulging eyes weren't an act. And the player he screamed at seemed to be taken back, more proof that his behavior was out of line.

Had Bunning let his competitive spirit get the better of him, or had something altered his state of mind? She enlarged the video more and zeroed in on the bottle he drank from—it was the sponsor's energy drink.

Hm.

An angry honk blared behind her, jarring her out of her thoughts. "Sorry," she said, waving her hand in apology.

As she pulled from the parking lot onto a side street, she tentatively activated the voice assistant on the phone—just like Prissy had taught her—and instructed the assistant to call Cooper Craft.

She was slightly amazed when she heard the call connect.

"Hi, Carlotta," Coop said. "This is a nice surprise."

"I'm glad you think so," she said. "Did I catch you at a bad time?"

"Not at all—what are you into?"

"I just dropped Prissy at her first day of school."

"How did that go?"

"Not well. I think she hates me."

"She doesn't hate you, she's just nervous and she's lashing out at you."

"I suppose. Mother is having a bad day, so that didn't help. I hope the doctor you found for her will at least be able to diagnose her."

"I hope so too."

"So... there is another reason I called."

"I'm listening."

"I was reviewing video on my phone from Saturday night's game."

"Uh-huh," he said, sounding wary.

"And I realized I caught Lewis Bunning's collapse."

"Uh-huh," he said, sounding more wary.

"He was drinking an energy drink just before it happened. I just wondered if it could've triggered his heart attack?"

"If he drank enough of them, sure. Large amounts of caffeine consumed in a short period of time can induce lethal cardiac arrhythmia. But Bunning's tox screen came back and his caffeine levels were way below the danger level."

"Did you find anything else that could've caused his heart attack?"

Coop sighed. "Where is this going, Carlotta?"

"Nowhere," she said. "Just wondering why a young and outwardly healthy young man would collapse and die."

"Unfortunately, it happens sometimes."

"Okay," she said lightly. "I just wanted to tell you about the video and the energy drink in case they were important."

"Thanks. But there's no evidence of anything ominous about Mr. Bunning's death."

"So you did run a full tox screen?"

He sighed. "Carlotta."

"What?"

"Are you bored?"

She frowned. "No." Then she sighed. "Maybe."

He gave a little laugh. "When do you go back to work?"

"Tomorrow."

"Good. I'll see you Thursday. Meanwhile, it's nice of you to be concerned, but put Mr. Bunning out of your mind."

She ended the call and, as Coop had suggested, mentally hit Delete on Lewis Bunning. She had too many other things to think about, like what was waiting for her when she returned to Neiman's.

Hopefully plus ten.

CHAPTER 9

"WELCOME BACK," General Store Manager Lindy Russell said.

Carlotta smiled. "Thank you. And thank you for being so patient while I sorted some personal matters. I assume you've heard at least the highlights."

Lindy nodded. "I can't imagine how hard it's been on you all this time with your parents missing, and the gossip you had to deal with, and raising your brother, too."

"My job here helped me to cope with everything... and to stay afloat financially. But now with all that behind me, I'm eager to talk about the new responsibilities you mentioned before I left for Vegas."

Lindy cleared her throat. "Yes, I'm eager to talk about that, too. But first, there's a personnel matter we need to address."

Carlotta's pulse blipped. "Personnel matter?"

Lindy stood and walked to her office door, then opened it. "You can come in now," she said to someone in the hall.

Carlotta turned to see Patricia Alexander standing in the doorway. Her stomach knotted. She and the blonde had never clicked, and when she discovered the young woman's parents had lost everything in the Ponzi-scheme blamed on her father, their work relationship had been even more awkward. Secretly Carlotta had been hoping the new assignment Lindy had hinted at would take her off the floor and away from Patricia.

"What's this about?" Carlotta asked, steeling herself to hear that Patricia had filed a grievance against her.

"Patricia has something she wants to tell you," Lindy said, then I'll decide where to go from here.

Carlotta dipped her chin. Patricia's expression was unreadable. As always, she was dressed in country club chic attire that, in Carlotta's opinion, aged her ten years, but she was a product of her upbringing... and she did have good taste.

Patricia took the chair next to Carlotta's and it was then Carlotta noticed the woman's hands were shaking—and sans her engagement ring. So the wedding to the baseball player was off?

"I..." Patricia began, then stopped. "I came to work at Neiman's under false pretenses."

Carlotta frowned. "What do you mean?"

Her throat convulsed. "Someone in the D.A.'s office approached me about working here—with you—in case you let it slip where your parents were hiding out."

Shock knifed through her chest. "You were working for the D.A. as an informant?"

Patricia grimaced. "If it's any consolation, I didn't really tell them anything."

"Because I didn't know where my parents were!"

"And that's what I kept telling them."

Carlotta touched her hand to her forehead, trying to absorb the news.

"Obviously, I didn't know about this," Lindy said. "Otherwise, I would never have hired Patricia."

"The thing is," Patricia rushed to say, "I really like working here, and I came to admire how you handle yourself, Carlotta. I realize now it couldn't have been easy after your parents left, with everyone assuming your father had done the things he was accused of." She wet her lips. "My family included."

Carlotta didn't say anything. At different times, hadn't she also believed her father was guilty?

"You can go now, Patricia," Lindy said. "You and I will talk later."

Patricia looked miserable. "I really am sorry, Carlotta, for thinking the worst of your family. No matter what happens, I hope you can forgive me." She stood and quickly left the room.

When the door closed, Lindy heaved a sigh. "Well, this is awkward. My first instinct was to fire Patricia. But in light of the fact that she has a stellar work record and she brought me this information voluntarily, I decided I would leave it up to you."

Carlotta blinked. "Me?"

"Yes. You're the one affected by Patricia's presence here. If you want me to let her go, I'll do it today, and she'll never know you had anything to do with it."

Carlotta felt an unfamiliar sensation wash over her—power. Most of her adult life she'd felt powerless over the circumstances of her life, but the results of the last few weeks had proved what she could do when she put her mind to it, including finding her parents—something the D.A., Jack, and even the FBI hadn't been able to do. She'd taken back her power, and it was a heady feeling.

The question was, what would she do with it?

"Can I have some time to think about it?" she asked.

"Of course. Meanwhile, let's talk about your next step with Neiman's."

"I'm listening," Carlotta said.

"How would you feel about running the bridal salon?"

Carlotta squinted. "In Dallas?" The Neiman-Marcus bridal salon was world-famous.

Lindy sat forward. "Actually, we're building a second salon here in Atlanta… and we want you to run it."

Pleasured astonishment washed over her. "Me?"

Lindy smiled and nodded. "You're the clear choice. You have the floor experience, the sales record, and you have

71

impeccable taste. You've demonstrated loyalty to Neiman's and shown strong leadership skills. And you know the Atlanta market."

Carlotta was reeling trying to take it all in. "I don't know what to say."

"I hope you'll say yes." Lindy opened a file and slid a sheet of paper toward Carlotta. "Here's the basic offer."

Carlotta glanced over the terms and felt her jaw go slack. A director title and more than twice what she would make in a great sales year.

"I don't mean to rush you," Lindy said, "but with the extra time you've taken off, we're bumping up against construction deadlines. And ideally, I'd like for you to have input into the salon buildout."

"This I don't have to think about," Carlotta said, feeling positively giddy. "I accept."

Lindy smiled wide. "Excellent. I think together we'll make the salon a star asset for the company. As a director, you'll have an assistant working under you, but they'll be your right hand. Human resources will post the job right away unless you have someone internally in mind."

What had Randolph said? *Forgive and forget—then start over.*

"Actually, I do have an internal candidate in mind…. Patricia Alexander."

CHAPTER 10

"HOW IS YOUR ANXIETY level?" E. asked.

Wes pressed his foot into the floor to stop his leg from jumping. "Fine."

"So no drug cravings?"

"Nope." Not in the last thirty seconds or so. Exacerbated by the cash Randolph had given him that was burning a hole in his pocket—and his soul.

She nodded her approval. E. seemed much improved over last week. Her auburn hair was long and loose, her makeup was flawless, and she was wearing a lavender silk blouse he hadn't seen before.

"How is the home repair project going with your Dad?"

"Good." Not good. Every time he drove in a nail, Randolph pulled it out and did it again—the right way. Wes examined his hands, found a tiny bit of nail left on his right middle finger, and proceeded to chew it off.

"And how is your mother?"

Distant and cold. It was as if she realized Wes was someone she should know, but since she couldn't reconcile him with any trustworthy memory, she didn't want him around. "We're taking her to see a new doctor tomorrow."

She smiled. "I'll be hoping for the best."

"Thanks." There was a hangnail on his left pinky, so he munched it off, too.

"There's no news from the D.A.'s office on the Vegas charges. Just be aware your ankle monitor is on twenty-four-seven. If you leave Fulton County, you could be arrested and hauled back to Nevada."

He nodded.

"By the way, Richard McCormick called. He said he offered you a job."

"Oh... yeah."

"You weren't going to tell me?"

His father's words came back to him. "Why would I want to work in a cubicle in a stuffy city building?"

"Do you have a better offer? I thought you quit your courier job."

His cover for doing collections with Mouse. "I did."

"And you haven't been working for the morgue lately."

"Right." Coop had been so busy doing autopsies, he hadn't been doing much body moving.

"So?" she prompted.

"So I haven't told McCormick no."

She sat back in her chair. "Okay. I know you have a lot on your mind. That's all for this week."

He pushed to his feet and slung his backpack to his shoulder.

"Before you go," she said, pulling out a drawer, "I need a urine sample." She set a paper cup and lid on the corner of her desk.

Wes frowned. "I told you, I'm clean."

"Good. Then the drug test will confirm it."

He picked it up, squashing a spike of frustration. At least taking a whizz was easier than giving blood.

"And Wes... have you given any thought to my suggestion of talking to a family therapist? Even if the rest of your family doesn't want to, you might benefit going alone."

"Thanks, but that's not necessary."

"Okay. I'll see you next week. Check in with Officer Scott at the men's restroom."

He started to leave.

"Wes, you forgot your cooler."

His heartrate spiked, but he calmly walked back to pick up the blue neoprene bag. "Thanks."

She smiled. "I shouldn't have said anything—I forgot to pack my lunch. Anything good in there?"

"Naw. Just a couple of sodas."

"Have a good day."

He left her office, then walked to the men's restroom where Officer Scott checked out his wiener while he peed in the cup.

It was the only action his wiener had been getting lately. With Liz locked up and Meg freezing him out, he was back to do-it-yourself sex. After he'd made good on the two hundred bucks he "owed" her, Alexis in Vegas had told him to call her if he was ever in town, but he still had a bad taste in his mouth over the whole Vegas experience, finding his parents notwithstanding.

And for someone who'd dreamed of being in the World Series of Poker, that said a lot.

As he left the building, he checked his phone—still a few minutes to kill before Mouse was supposed to be there. He tapped over to messages on the off chance Meg had made contact.

Nope.

Maybe it was for the best. He'd hoped that with his family reassembled, Meg would see him as more normal, with more to offer a young woman who was destined to do big things. But his family wasn't turning out to be the cozy support system he'd expected.

The urge for a hit of Oxy struck him like a zap of static electricity. He opened the cooler and removed a cold energy drink, cracked it open and downed it, then crushed the can in his hand to feel the zing of pain. The urge passed… this time.

STEPHANIE BOND

A familiar black Town Car pulled up to the curb and the driver side window zoomed down to reveal Mouse's ugly mug. "Hiya, Little Man."

Wes grinned. "Hey, Mouse." He handed him the cooler. "Here's the money I owe The Carver… and it's real this time."

Mouse unzipped the cooler and looked inside. "All I see is a Red Bull."

"It's on the bottom."

The big man pulled out a block of clear ice with the stack of bills Randolph had given Wes suspended in the middle. "That's different."

Putting the cash on ice was the only way Wes had been able to not blow the money on cards—or worse.

"It's all there," Wes said. "This should get me square."

Mouse put the block of ice back in the cooler then extended it to Wes. "You're already square with The Carver."

Wes frowned. "How's that?'

Mouse pursed his thick lips. "Call it my thank you for the call from Vegas tipping me off about the feds moving in on Dillon. It gave me time to distance myself."

Wes blinked. "You're welcome, Mouse, but I didn't expect any repayment."

"You got it anyway."

He pulled his hand over his mouth to wipe away the stupid flood of emotion. Mouse had done a lot for him—helped him get off oxy, had given him advice, and now this. "Thanks, man."

"You're welcome."

"You could've told me on the phone," Wes said, "instead of making the trip down here."

Mouse nodded. "Yeah." Then held up a brown bag with dark grease stains. "But then who's gonna help me eat these burgers?"

Wes grinned. "I can help you out."

"Get in."

He walked around and climbed into the passenger seat.

76

Mouse drove the big car to the far side of the parking lot and killed the engine. Wes pulled out the burgers and fries and they dug in.

"How's it going?" Mouse asked. "I'm happy for you that your dad is back."

"Thanks. But how upset is The Carver that Dillon's in jail?"

"Between you and me, notsomuch. That boy has been such a pain in the ass to his old man, I think The Carver is relieved that he's going away for a while. Might straighten him up."

Wes gave a little laugh. "Wow, so even the son of a loan shark can disappoint his dad."

Mouse frowned. "Everything okay with you and your dad?"

Wes shrugged. "It's just different than I thought it would be. We don't have much in common."

"That's not so unusual for fathers and sons."

"I guess so. We just have different ideas about my future."

"What does he want you to do?"

"Something in business that makes a lot of money."

Mouse nodded. "What do you want to do?"

Wes hesitated. "You're gonna laugh."

"Try me."

"I'd like to be a doctor."

Mouse grinned. "That's great, Little Man."

"Yeah, but it takes years of college, and I'm already behind other kids my age."

"So, you'll make it up."

"But I might not even be able to get in, with all the trouble I've been in."

"Still, you should try."

Wes looked over. "Yeah?"

"Yeah."

Wes bit into a fry and chewed happily. *Yeah.*

CHAPTER 11

BY THE TIME Carlotta stepped off the elevator and into the hall outside the neurologist's office with Valerie and Birch, she was exhausted and ready to fly apart at the seams. Getting Prissy ready and dropped off at school had been its usual struggle, and convincing her mother to leave the house had proved to be harder than she'd anticipated. Valerie kept asking for Randolph who had waltzed through the kitchen early, looking dapper and dropping kisses, then dashed off with the vague explanation of needing to take care of a business matter before the appointment. He assured Carlotta he would meet them at the doctor's office.

But they could've used his help to calm Valerie for the trip to the medical center. She seemed to think they were trying to kidnap her, and only cooperated when Birch told her they were taking her to see Randolph.

Except the only person waiting for them was Coop, looking handsome and professional in slacks and a sport coat.

"Good morning," he said, chipper as always.

Carlotta wanted to collapse into him and have a good cry. She didn't trust her voice, could only nod. He must have sensed her emotional state because he immediately turned to Valerie and offered a charming smile.

"Hi, Valerie. I've been waiting for you. I'm so glad you're here."

Valerie instantly thawed. "Well, hello. Aren't you nice and tall?"

Valerie had been enamored of Coop from the start, had even offered to take off her clothes for an examination when Carlotta had smuggled him into the Vegas house to check her mother's general well-being.

"Why, thank you." Coop offered her his arm. "May I escort you in to meet a friend?"

"Of course," Valerie said, tucking her hand into the crook of his arm. "Any friend of yours is a friend of mine."

The elevator door opened, and Carlotta's hopes rose that Randolph had arrived. Instead Wes stepped out, combing his wind-swept hair with his hands and sporting a nice shirt, bless him. Carlotta knew their mother's indifference toward him had to cut deep, but he'd handled it like a grownup.

Valerie stopped when she saw Wes. She glared. "What's he doing here?"

A shadow passed over Wes's eyes, and Carlotta's heart squeezed for him.

"I asked him to come," Coop said quickly.

Valerie looked back to Coop, then smiled. "What's your name?"

"Cooper Craft, ma'am."

"Oh, yes, that's right. Carlotta wrote your name on a wall underneath where I'd written mine."

Carlotta's breath caught.

Coop glanced at her, eyebrows raised.

She shook her head as if she had no idea what her mother was talking about. Coop let it go, steering her mother toward the waiting room.

She exhaled, thinking she'd probably go to hell for pretending a dementia patient was making up something rather than cop to a weak moment of romanticism.

Birch followed Coop and Valerie, leaving her and Wes alone.

She reached forward to straighten his collar. "I'm sorry about that."

He shrugged. "Mom's sick."

"Yes. She does love you, you know."

He gave her a rueful smile. "The nine-year-old me anyway."

"You look nice. Thanks for coming."

He stabbed at his glasses. "I wanted to. Where's Dad?"

"He left early this morning, said he'd meet us here. He's not at the townhouse?"

"No. I haven't seen him."

A ribbon of unease unfurled in her stomach. What was Randolph up to?

"Come on, let's go in," she said. Today was all about their mother.

A few minutes spent in the general waiting room was a sobering experience. One wall was covered with take-away pamphlets on Alzheimer's, Lewy bodies dementia, ALS, Parkinson's disease, Huntington's disease, and more. Patients in various stages of decline sat with their caretakers, some seemingly lucid and aware, but others with slack expressions and unfocused eyes. Fear crowded Carlotta's chest. Some diseases robbed people of their mobility and independence and dignity. It was no way for anyone to live... or die.

Stuck in her mind was a casual comment Hannah had made when she'd told her friend her mother was suffering from dementia.

Your mother is awfully young for dementia, isn't she? That doesn't bode well for you...

Because it only took one glance at her and Valerie to see she'd received most of her DNA from her mother. There was none of Randolph in her... ditto for Priscilla.

Coop touched her arm. "Are you okay?"

"I was just thinking... if Mom's disease is genetic, what does the future hold for me and Wes and Prissy?"

"Don't go there," he said gently. "We don't even know what we're dealing with yet."

We.

She felt a rush of gratitude and yes, *love* for this man who had always stepped up and stepped in to help, and asked for nothing in return. "You're right, of course. Thank you for making this possible, and for being here."

"I'm glad I could. Is Randolph coming?"

"He's supposed to."

"The doctor is ready to see Valerie. Should we wait?"

Carlotta sighed. "Maybe he's stuck in traffic. Let me call him." She punched in Randolph's number and listened to it ring four times before it rolled over to voice mail. "Dad... where are you? We're walking in to see the doctor now." She ended the call, her frustration ballooning. How could he not be here for Valerie? For her and Wes? Nothing could be more important today.

A fantastical thought slipped into her brain. Had Randolph left again, now that her mother and Prissy were in good hands? Was he chafing under the obligation of his reunited family? Now that he'd cleared his name, had he decided to escape the awful inevitability of his wife's deterioration and live his life elsewhere?

"Carlotta?"

Coop was staring at her, looking concerned. "No, we're not waiting."

He inclined his head. "Okay. Whenever you're ready."

Coop had arranged for them to have a private meeting room to meet the doctor and discuss Valerie's case before she was examined. He volunteered to sit with Valerie while Carlotta, Wes, and Birch conferred with the neurologist.

The room they were led to was cheery, if small. Bright colored upholstered chairs surrounded a white table. The vase of live flowers in the middle were a nice touch, but she didn't miss the box of tissues sitting next to it. It was a room designed for delivering bad news in the best possible environment.

On the walls hung colorful framed paintings, some more abstract than others, but all revealing an above-average grasp of composition and color. They were so arresting, she moved closer to examine them and the names of the artists. To her surprise, they were all dementia patients, most of them suffering from Alzheimer's.

So apparently creativity was one dimension of human consciousness that even dementia couldn't squash entirely. It was a positive thought to hang on to.

The door opened and an attractive bespectacled woman wearing a lab coat entered, carrying a file folder labeled WREN, V.

"Hello, I'm Dr. Cullum. You're the family of Valerie Wren?"

"That's right," Carlotta said, stepping forward. "I'm her daughter, Carlotta. This is my brother, Wesley, and this is Birch, my mother's caretaker for the past two years."

The doctor shook hands all around. "Will Mrs. Wren's husband be joining us?"

"Not today," Carlotta murmured. "Thank you for agreeing to see our mother."

She smiled. "Dr. Craft was very persuasive, and this is an unusual case. I'm happy to help if I can. Why don't we all sit?"

They each found a chair around the table. Dr. Cullum steepled her hands, then addressed Carlotta and Wes. "I understand Mrs. Wren has been in hiding with your father for almost ten years?"

Carlotta nodded. "And we have a nine-year-old sister who was living with them."

Dr. Cullum opened the file and made some notes. "So Mrs. Wren has been living under an assumed name?"

"Right—Melanie Rudolph."

She made another note. "And where does she reside at the moment?"

"In the house where Carlotta and I grew up," Wes supplied.

"And that seems to be the time period where she is, um, stuck," Carlotta said. "My younger sister resembles me, so my mother often calls her by my name."

"And she thinks I'm still a nine-year-old boy, upstairs in my room," Wes said.

The doctor nodded. "It's not uncommon for dementia patients to revert to old memories. There's a medical explanation, but suffice to say those are simply the memories they've had the longest and have recalled more often, even before they were ill."

"So first in, first out?" Wes said.

"Exactly."

"What happens today?" Carlotta asked.

"Mrs. Wren will undergo a series of tests. We'll be doing a basic physical exam to assess her general health, including collecting blood and urine samples. We'll also be testing her muscle strength, coordination, vision, hearing, and sensation... and a mental status test to see how aware she is of her surroundings, time and place, that sort of thing. And a memory test, both short term and long-term." She slid papers across the table. "I'll need some information to base those questions on, the dates both of you were born, that kind of thing. And here's a rather lengthy form for Mrs. Wren's medical history."

"We might not be able to provide much," Carlotta warned. "Birch has medical records for the past two years, but I'll have to get my father to fill in the gaps." *If I can find him.*

The doctor nodded. "As much as you can provide, the more information, the better. Can you tell me if your mother ever had any substance abuse issues?"

Carlotta exchanged a glance with Wesley. "She abused alcohol when we were younger. My father told me she got sober when she found out she was pregnant with our sister, and has been sober ever since."

Dr. Cullum made more notes. "Okay, that's helpful. Anything else you can think of that seems pertinent?"

Carlotta searched her memory. "My sister said Valerie started forgetting things when she was six, so that would've been about three years ago."

"Okay. And this was while she was living Las Vegas, Nevada?"

"Yes."

The doctor kept jotting. "Any injuries?"

Carlotta looked to Birch, but he shook his head. "Randolph would know more, but he never mentioned anything to me."

"I'll find out and get back to you," Carlotta said

"Okay, that's all for now. Give the paperwork to a nurse when you're finished. Your mother is agitated, but we'll try to get through as many tests today as we can. Then, depending on what we find, we might schedule follow up tests and imaging." She stood and flashed them a hopeful smile. "Please be patient. Sometimes we have answers right away, and sometimes it takes a while."

When the doctor opened the door to leave, the sound of Valerie's raised, panicked voice reached Carlotta's ears. She leapt up and followed the doctor to an exam room where Valerie was resisting a nurse who was trying to take her blood pressure. Coop was attempting to calm her, but Valerie was wild-eyed and flailing. "Get away from me! I'm supposed to meet my husband, where are you hiding him?"

Birch and Carlotta stepped closer, each trying to soothe her, but she was inconsolable.

"Where is my husband? *Where is my husband?*"

Carlotta fought back tears. Had her mother's disease progressed too far for her to even tolerate the tests?

Footsteps sounded at the door. "Here I am, dear."

Carlotta turned to see Randolph walk into the room, handsome and composed and smiling at Valerie. They parted to give him a clear path to her.

Valerie's eyes lighted on him and she was transformed. "Randolph, my love... where have you been?"

"It doesn't matter," he said, clasping her hands in his. "I'm here now."

She glanced around the room. "Who are all these people?"

"Friends," Randolph said. "They're going to help you. You need to do what they say, alright?"

"Alright," she agreed. Then she bit into her lip. "Are you leaving me?"

Carlotta's breath caught at the anguish in Valerie's voice.

"No," Randolph said, patting her hand. "I'll be right beside you."

Valerie looked happy and relieved. "Good."

Carlotta's throat clogged with emotion. It was remarkable to see how devoted her mother was to her father. And Randolph had come through... today.

She moved toward the door and Wes, Birch, and Coop followed.

Coop closed the door behind him, and they all exhaled.

"Now what?" Wes asked.

"Now we wait," Coop said, turning back toward the main waiting room. "This could take a while."

"I saw a sign for a vending room down the hall," Birch said. "Wes, why don't we go get everyone some coffee?" He glanced at Carlotta. "Then we'll tackle those medical history forms."

She nodded gratefully.

Coop watched them walk away, then looked back to her. "What's Birch's story?"

She followed him to two empty chairs and sat down, feeling drained. "I don't know all the details, but I think he has a military background. Randolph hired him to watch Mom and Prissy when he wasn't around, primarily as a body guard. Then as Mom's condition worsened, he became more of a caretaker. But he saved us all from Liz Fischer."

"And then you saved Liz," Coop said, referring to her decision to pull Liz from the burning house.

"I couldn't just let her and her baby die."

"I know Jack is grateful," he said. "Have you seen him lately?" His tone was light, but she wondered if he was fishing for a clue as to where things stood between her and Jack.

"A couple of times," she admitted. And she'd be lying if she said hadn't thought about his declaration that he hadn't told her things he should have. "But considering everything Jack has on his plate, I don't expect to be seeing much of him from now on."

Coop made a thoughtful noise. "And how's Peter?"

"I went to visit him in jail a few days ago. It was depressing, but he hopes to be released on bail soon." She gave a little laugh. "He'll probably sell my engagement ring to help with that."

"And you'd be okay with that?"

"Yes."

He didn't comment, but the corners of his mouth turned up a bit. "And how is Miss Priscilla?"

Carlotta groaned. "The same. I'm trying to be patient. She's dealing with a lot right now."

"About that... I was wondering what you'd think about me getting Prissy a puppy? I remember her saying she'd like to have one."

Carlotta made a rueful sound. "That's so sweet of you, Coop, honestly... but right now I don't think we can handle one more thing. But maybe later, when things settle down?"

"Okay, sure."

"Hannah has another roller derby match Saturday—do you want to meet us there?"

"Yeah, sounds good. Maybe we can have that ice cream date afterward." Then he cleared his throat. "By the way, I've been meaning to tell you... after you called me the other day about Lewis Bunning's behavior just before he died, I decided to run a more in-depth tox screen."

She arched an eyebrow. "And?"

"And I found SPICE in his system."

"What's that?"

"It's known on the street as synthetic marijuana, although since it doesn't actually contain THC, it doesn't show up on a normal tox screen."

"You can die from this stuff?"

"Absolutely. Most people have no idea how dangerous it is. It's basically herbs sprayed with synthetic cannabis substance," he said, using air quotes. "But frankly, it can be sprayed with anything that induces a buzz, including commercial pesticides."

"It's smoked?"

"Or ingested, as in this case. He washed it down with the energy drink you mentioned, or more probably, mixed it in."

She nodded. "That particular brand is known for having herbs and fruit in the bottle—that's why their slogan is 'Shake things up.' Was the combination what made it deadly?"

"No. The caffeine in the energy drink would've helped to speed it through his system, but the SPICE did him in. The extra problem with ingesting it versus smoking it or chewing it like gum is the buzz takes longer to kick in, and if there's a bad reaction, the person already has it in their body, so it's almost too late to do anything about it."

"Do you think that's why he was acting so aggressively before he collapsed?"

"Probably."

Carlotta winced. "So Lewis Bunning thought he was going to get a buzz, and he got a heart attack instead?"

Coop nodded. "Sad, huh? But now at least I can file a report so law enforcement can be on the lookout for more of it." He smiled. "So... good catch. You probably saved some lives."

She smiled. "So you're going to listen to me from now on?"

"I can't promise that, but I like the sound of 'from now on.'"

His gaze was intense, sending shards of sudden awareness through her chest. Her lips parted, but she was spared from responding by the return of Wes and Birch, juggling coffees.

But he'd certainly given her a lot to think about.

CHAPTER 12

WES STIFLED A YAWN, then leaned forward in the waiting room chair to stretch his back. It had been a long, tiring day. The rest of the neurology patients were gone. The fact that his mother was still being examined could be a good thing, he told himself.

Or a bad thing.

He was still marveling over the earlier scene where his dad had walked into the room when his mom was freaking out, and instantly, she was better. That was so cool. If he could have that with someone someday, his life would be complete.

Who was he kidding? Not with someone—with Meg. But before they could grow old and senile together, he needed to convince her to go out with him.

Randolph came out of the exam area into the waiting room looking a little less polished than when he'd arrived—the day had taken a toll on him as well.

Wes stood and walked over to the reception desk where his father had stopped.

"Is Mom done?"

"Yes," Randolph said, glancing around the empty waiting room.

"Carlotta had to go pick up Prissy from school, and Birch went with her to get dinner started. Coop had to get back to the morgue, so I thought I'd stick around to, you know, see if I could… help."

His dad's smile made the hours of waiting worthwhile. "Thanks, son. Your mom will be out in a few minutes. I still need to fill out these forms for insurance," he said, gesturing to a pile of paper. Do you want to bring the car around to the front of the medical center?"

"Sure," Wes said, holding out his hand for the keys.

Randolph handed over the key to his new Mercedes SUV. "It's on the third floor of the parking garage."

Wes nodded, then jogged out into the hall, happy to be useful.

He heard Meg's voice and smelled her citrusy perfume just before she and her lab-coated father came around the corner. She saw him and stopped. "Wes?"

"Hi."

Her father, Dr. Harold Vincent, was a big deal in the genetics field. He and Wes had crossed paths—and words—a few times during Wes's pursuit of Meg.

"Daddy, you remember Wesley Wren," Meg said.

Dr. Vincent's mouth flattened. "I sure do." His gaze darted to Wes's foot. "Nice ankle bracelet."

Wes glanced down to see his ankle monitor showing below his pants leg. Minus ten.

Then the man zeroed in on the big honking Mercedes keychain Wes held. "Let me guess, you're here posing as a doctor and you managed to borrow his vehicle for a few hours?"

He was referring to the time Wes had stolen a doctor's lab coat and nametag in order to crash a lecture Dr. Vincent had given.

"Daddy," Meg said in a reproachful voice.

Wes stabbed at his glasses. "Uh, no."

The door to the waiting room opened and his parents appeared. His mom's hand was tucked contentedly around his dad's elbow, but her pretty face was lined with fatigue. His dad glanced at Meg and her father, then nodded politely.

"Dad, this is Meg Vincent," Wes said. "Meg and I work together at the city IT department. And this is her father, Dr. Harold Vincent."

Wes made eye contact with Meg. "These are my parents,

Randolph and Valerie Wren."

"Hello," Randolph said, stepping forward to shake hands with Meg and with her father, the latter of whom seemed muddled by the turn of events. His glance bounced to the sign on the door—Cognitive & Behavioral Neurology—and he straightened a bit.

Asshole.

"Hello, Mrs. Wren," Meg said, stepping forward.

Wes held his breath, not sure what to expect.

"Hello," his mother said with a smile. "Do I know you?"

"Wesley just introduced us, dear," Randolph said gently. "This is Meg."

"Wesley," his mother declared. "Now there's a nice name." She smiled at Meg. "If I ever have a son I'm going to name him Wesley."

Wes's face burned. He wasn't ashamed of his mother... just that he was so forgettable.

Meg's eyes clouded, then she recovered. "Yes, Wesley is a name any son would be proud to have."

He appreciated that Meg talked to his mother as if she were well.

Randolph tried to steer Valerie toward the elevator, but now she seemed captivated by Meg. "You are a *lovely* girl."

"Thank you," Meg said.

"You're welcome," Valerie said, then she frowned. "Do I know you?"

Randolph patted her hand. "It's time to go, dear. Wes, did you already bring the car around?"

"Not yet."

"It's our fault," Meg said quickly. "We were keeping him. We'll let you go, Wes. It was so nice to meet you," she said to his parents.

"Same here," Randolph said congenially.

"Goodbye," Valerie said in a lilting voice.

"Have a good evening," Dr. Vincent murmured as they walked

by.

Wes punched the elevator button and watched them walk away. When they reached the end of the hallway, Meg looked back at him and smiled.

It was something.

CHAPTER 13

"I FIGURED the wedding expo would have cured you of wanting to work with brides," Hannah said from the driver's seat of her van.

"It's a big promotion," Carlotta said from the passenger seat. "And a great opportunity."

"And you picked that starchy Barbie doll Patricia to be your assistant? Are you a glutton for punishment?"

"Maybe," Carlotta said with a laugh. "So far it's working out, though. She seems eager to please." Because Patricia felt guilty for agreeing to spy on her for the D.A.?

"Yeah, well, Miss Director, are you going to have to work late every Saturday?"

"For a while, at least until the buildout is finished." She checked her phone for the time. "Am I going to make you late?"

"No. We still have time to stop and pick up Babs. She's the blocker I'm standing in for—she broke her leg earlier this season and hasn't been to any matches since, but she's dying to. That's why I drove the van."

Plus she probably didn't want the roller derby girls to know her other car was an Audi roadster convertible.

"I probably could've made it home in traffic to get Wes and Prissy," Carlotta said, "but I was kind of hoping you and I would get some time alone."

"Aw," Hannah said. "I fucking love you, too. How are they

getting there? Did Shithead get his driver's license back yet?"

"No. Wes said he asked Chance to swing by, but he couldn't."

"Um, yeah, he had something to do tonight."

"So Coop is going to swing by and get them."

Hannah's jet black eyebrows shot up. "Coop? What's that about?" she asked in a sing-songy voice.

"Don't jump to conclusions. He's just doing me a favor."

"Uh-huh, like finding a neurologist for your mom. He seems to be insinuating himself into the Wren family."

"You know Coop—he's just a nice guy."

"Yeah, but he's especially nice to *you*. Why don't you sleep with the poor man already and put him out of his misery? Besides, now that I'm married, the only way I'm going to get to have sex with Coop is vicariously through you."

Carlotta laughed, but she was glad to hear that Hannah took her vows seriously—ironic considering she used to only sleep with married men.

Was it possible that everyone was growing up a little?

"Have you heard back from your mother's tests?" Hannah asked.

"We have to take her back Monday for followup imaging... I have no idea if that's a good or a bad sign. Coop says it's neither."

"Try to be optimistic," Hannah said. "Drugs are better these days—and you never know, a cure for whatever she has could be just around the corner."

Carlotta nodded. Intellectually, she comprehended all of those things, but emotionally, she was on a rollercoaster. "Speaking of drugs, did you tell the rest of the team about the SPICE Coop found in Lewis Bunning's system?"

"Yeah," Hannah said. "Everyone was surprised. Lewis was a little odd, but he wasn't someone who got high or even drank beer at the after-game parties."

"What do you mean by odd?"

Hannah grunted. "A couple of the girls said they caught him

93

hiding in the locker room, watching them change."

"That's more than odd, that's predatory."

"Okay, yeah. But it's not what you think. Lewis was gay."

"Why would a gay man hide to watch women change?"

"He said he liked the stockings and the makeup and stuff."

"He was a cross-dresser?"

"A wannabe, trying to work up the nerve. So maybe he thought SPICE would make it easier, you know?"

"Coop said people can die from it the first time they use it."

"Yeah, Chance said it's dodgy stuff."

"Well, he would know," Carlotta said lightly.

Hannah turned to look at her. "I know what he does on the side, but he mostly sells weed and uppers."

Carlotta gave her a pointed look.

"Okay, and some downers and Ritalin and generic Viagra. And a little bit of Oxy... but that's all. He said he'd never mess with SPICE or bath salts or any of that crap."

"So he's a discerning drug dealer."

"Yeah—he has standards." Then Hannah sighed. "But his business is part of the reason I don't want to live with him. My father would murder me if I got caught in a drug raid."

"So you and Chance are always going to live apart?"

"No. He's going to quit selling drugs and go legit."

"Doing what?"

"We're still considering our options. I'll keep you posted."

"Okay, well if anyone on the roller derby team knows where Lewis got the SPICE, they need to go to the police. More people could die."

"I'll spread the word."

"You don't think he could've gotten it from someone on the team?"

"A big fat no there. The team has a zero tolerance for illegal substances. And the coach is so opposed to stimulants and sugar, she has a no soda, no coffee, no tea policy on the day of the matches, and will only let us have energy drinks and Gatorade at half-time. She runs a tight ship."

Hannah put on her blinker to turn left into an apartment complex.

The shabby two-story building featured room doors facing the outside, with lots of concrete and metal stairs.

"It looks like it used to be a hotel."

"I think it was."

Carlotta scanned their surroundings. "Isn't it a little dark around here?"

Hannah nodded. "This is a dicey pocket of town, but I'm sure the rent is cheap."

"It's nice of you to do this," Carlotta offered.

"The roller derby girls are good people. Everyone looks out for everyone else... it's nice, you know? Kind of like what you and I have."

"Aw," Carlotta said. "I fucking love you, too."

Hannah laughed and pulled the van around to the rear of the complex and parked.

"The elevator is out, so I told Babs I'd help her navigate the stairs with her crutches." She glanced around the shadowy parking lot. "I think you should come with me rather than wait in the car."

Carlotta was already climbing out.

Hannah locked the van doors, then walked to the center stairs. "Babs lives in 203," she said, jogging up the steps.

"Does she live alone?" Carlotta lagged behind her since she was still wearing work clothes.

"I think so. She's divorced."

When they reached her paint-peeling door, Carlotta silently counted her blessings that she'd never had to live in a place so desolate.

Hannah knocked on the door, then frowned when it swung open a few inches. The interior was dark.

Hannah gave Carlotta a worried look, then put her hand on the knob and leaned inside. "Babs? It's Hannah Kizer and a friend. Your door was open."

When there was no response, Carlotta's pulse kicked up.

Hannah called out again... and again, no response.

Hannah pulled out her phone and turned on a light. "Wait here."

"No way, I'm right behind you," Carlotta said, turning on her phone light, too. She walked in behind Hannah and detected a faint scent that burned her nose. Hannah swiped at light switches on walls, illuminating a small living room, then an eat-in kitchen, all the while calling the woman's name.

"Hannah," Carlotta said, then pointed to a desk whose drawers had been pulled out and their contents dumped. Ditto for kitchen cabinet drawers. The place had been tossed.

Hannah slowly advanced to the bedroom. The door was ajar, the interior black. She stuck her hand inside and felt around the corner for a light switch, then suddenly the room was bathed with light. They both gasped.

A bleach-blond woman lay on the bed dressed in a Bruised Peaches uniform, sans the helmet and equipment, and very obviously dead. Her pin-up girl makeup made her wide-open eyes and mouth even more dramatic. A crutch lay across her discolored neck, and its mate lay on the floor, broken.

"Is that Babs?" Carlotta whispered.

"Yeah. Fuck. You call Jack, and I'll call Coop."

"No, you call Jack, and I'll call Coop."

Hannah frowned. "Why don't I call the team coach, and you call both your lovers?"

Carlotta made a face, then called Coop first, hoping to intercept him before he reached the Buckhead house.

"Hi, there," he said, his voice warm and happy.

"Hi," she said. "This isn't a social call."

"What's up?"

"Hannah and I stopped to pick up one of her teammates... and found her strangled."

He made a sorrowful noise. "Jesus. Okay, I was on my way to pick up Wes and Prissy, but I'm turning around."

"I'll text Wes to let him know. Hannah's on the phone with the coach, so I suspect the match will be called off anyway."

"Okay. Is Jack on his way?"

"I'm calling him next."

"Oh… you called me first?"

She squinted at his implied pecking order.

"Not that it matters," he said quickly. "I'm on my way."

Carlotta ended the call and pulled up Jack's number. She hadn't phoned him directly since returning from Vegas. She wondered if he would think it was a personal call, and if he would even answer.

But he did, sounding fatigued.

"Hi, Carlotta. What are you into on a Saturday night?"

"Um… a crime scene?"

He sighed. "Of course you are. Is there a body?"

"Yes. A member of Hannah's roller derby team. We found her strangled in her apartment."

Another sigh. "Give me the address, and don't touch anything—and *no* pictures, got it?"

She made an irritated noise. "Okay."

"I'm sending uniforms to secure the scene—they'll probably beat me there. I'll call Coop on the way."

"I already called him."

"You called Coop first?"

Carlotta rolled her eyes.

"Not that it matters," he added quickly. "I'm on my way."

She ended the call, shaking her head.

Since Hannah was still on the phone, she scanned the scene to see if anything stood out. The drawers of a low dresser had been pulled out and the contents—clothes, from the look of it—had been ransacked. Everything else in the room seemed undisturbed.

The bed was made, but the bedspread was rumpled and dragging on the floor—Babs had struggled for her life. Carlotta bent down to examine the rubber bottom of the broken crutch, then stood when Hannah ended her call.

Her expression was pinched. "The coach is devastated. Babs was one of the co-founders of the team. She's calling off tonight's match."

"I'm sorry, Hannah, for you and your teammates."

"I didn't know Babs well, but she's best friends with the jammer you saw skate last week, Missy Fuller."

"Missy Behavin'?"

"Right. She wouldn't be able to skate tonight. This is going to be hard for everyone to take on the heels of Lewis's death."

Sirens sounded in the distance—the uniforms Jack had dispatched, she presumed. They walked back through the living room and elbowed their way out the front door as two Atlanta PD cars rolled up, lights flashing. They waved to get the cops' attention and told them where to find Babs. Two cops went inside, one began taping off the scene, and one started a report, asking for information on the victim. Neighbors peeked out windows and a few looky-loos gathered in the parking lot.

While Hannah talked to the officer, Carlotta leaned against the railing, thinking of the woman in her last moments of life. How awful to know you were going to die, that the final face you saw was a stranger, someone who had no idea if you were a good person, or what you meant to loved ones. When her finger touched something slimy, she pulled back, grimacing at the black streak. She found a tissue in her purse and wiped it off., then crossed her arms, resolved, as Jack had directed, not to touch anything.

As if she'd conjured him up, his car pulled into parking lot, and Coop was right behind him. They parked, then got out and shook hands in greeting. Then both men turned and looked up at her.

Carlotta sighed.

CHAPTER 14

"SQUARE YOUR HIPS," Randolph said. "And keep your eye on the ball."

Since Wes had no idea what squaring his hips meant, he focused on the golf ball on the ground near his feet, which hurt like hell from the new golf shoes his dad had given him. He lifted the club and swung wildly. Thankfully the head made contact this time, but the ball only made it a few yards down the green.

His father made a frustrated noise. "I assumed you'd been playing often."

"Not really," he mumbled. "Just swinging a driver." At the heads of late-paying customers of The Carver.

The disappointment he saw in his father's eyes was familiar—he remembered it from every time he'd struck out in Little League.

"Okay, well, I'll sign you up for lessons with the pro at the club."

At the thought of having to take lessons from some preppie dickhead for a sport he didn't particularly like, Wes considered taking the club he held and hitting himself in the head hard enough to just end it right there on the fairway.

His dad walked over to his own ball and took a stance.

Wes's phone vibrated. He glanced at the screen and when he saw it was a text from Meg, his damn heart danced.

I went to the roller derby match last night, but it was cancelled

He grinned. So she'd gone hoping to run into him.

One of the skaters was murdered in her apartment

Ugh, how horrible

Yeah... my sister and friend found her... was a bad scene

Just saying hi... see u soon

Ok

He put his phone away, feeling happy Meg had reached out.

"What's got you all smiles?" Randolph asked, walking back to his bag. Wes had missed his shot, but he was sure it had gone where it was supposed to.

"Uh... nothing."

His dad gave a laugh. "What's her name?"

Wes flushed. "Meg."

"Ah, the girl we ran into yesterday at the med center, the one you work with?"

"Yeah."

"Pretty girl. So you're dating or hooking up, or whatever kids call it these days?"

"Just hanging out sometimes."

"Good. She seemed age appropriate." A reference, no doubt, to Liz. "It's your swing. What club do you want?"

"You choose," Wes said. He couldn't tell them apart and he couldn't care less.

"Might as well try the seven iron," his dad said, handing him the club. "Square your hips, keep your eye on the ball, and this time, lock your elbows."

Wes assumed the position, swung the club... and whiffed it.

"Hey!" some guy in a foursome yelled behind them. "You're holding up play!"

Wes turned. "Hey, asshole—"

His father's hand on his shoulder stopped him. "Sorry about that," Randolph called in a friendly voice. "Got a virgin here. We'll move ahead."

Wes ground his teeth. Virgin?

"Pick up your bag, son, let's go to the next hole."

Wes put the rented club back in the rented bag. "We can just leave if you want. I'm pretty terrible."

Randolph laughed. "Yeah... but the only way to get better is to practice. And you need your own clubs. I'll make an appointment to have you fitted. I can use a new set myself."

Wes shouldered his bag, then trudged forward to match Randolph's stride, wincing against the pinch of the stiff shoes. He remembered the day Mouse had taken him golfing at a public course north of the city. They had both played lousy, hacking away at the ball and falling on the ground laughing at each other. It had been one of the best days of his life.

This was shaping up to be one of the worst.

"You'll get the hang of golf," Randolph said. At least I hope so, because it's going to be the family business."

Wes's head swung up. "Huh?"

"I did well as a day trader the last few years, but the market's gotten too volatile for good returns. And I don't want to get into hedge funds again, not at my age. So I've made an offer on a small driving range near Lindbergh, and I'd like you to help me run it."

He schooled his face to keep from showing how utterly unappealing that sounded. "No offense, Dad, but—"

"Hear me out," Randolph said. "It's a good, mostly cash business... and it would give us a legitimate business cover."

Wes frowned. "Cover for what?"

"To help launch your professional poker career."

Wes blinked. "Professional?"

"Yeah. Between my dealing skills and your eye for the cards, I think we can get you ready for the big leagues by the time you turn twenty-one. Until then, you can practice at casinos in Alaska, Minnesota, Wyoming, and Idaho, where it's legal to gamble at eighteen. No huge pots there, but you can hone your skills."

Wes was shocked his father would be willing to bet on him like that... and doubly shocked that he didn't feel more amped up about the prospect.

"Well, try to contain your excitement," Randolph said.

Wes wet his lips. "It's a great offer, Dad... but lately I've been thinking about going to school."

"But isn't the purpose of going to college to get a job making a lot of money when you get out?"

"Yeah, I guess."

"Have you seen the pots on the professional gambling circuit lately? If you're as good as I think you could be, you could retire before you're thirty."

Wes nodded. "It's just that... well, I think I'd like to go to medical school."

Randolph's eyes widened. "Medical school?"

"Yeah... I've really enjoyed working with Coop, and seeing how ill Mom is, well, I feel like maybe I could make a difference."

Randolph gave a little laugh. "Son, I know you're smart, but face facts—you're already at least two years behind the curve, and you have a police record."

Wes frowned. "I have a record because I hacked into the courthouse database to try to find information about your case."

"Really? I understood it was to fix speeding tickets for you and your friends."

He hardened his jaw. "I did that, but I left a backdoor so I could get back in to do a more thorough search."

Randolph nodded. "Well, I appreciate what you tried to do, but I doubt college admission boards will be as sympathetic."

His shoulders fell, along with his confidence.

"And I hesitate to mention it, but one of the conversations between you and Carlotta I overheard was about your compulsion for Oxycontin."

The air rushed out of Wes's lungs as if he'd been kicked. "That's... all over." Although even as he said it, he conceded a little rush at the mere mention of the drug.

"I hope so," Randolph said. "But if it isn't and you're caught, you'll never be allowed to practice medicine. And medical school is expensive... that's a big gamble to take on something you might not get to finish."

Wes's heart thudded in his chest. "I can be a doctor if I want to. I don't need your help."

Randolph made a rueful noise. "I'm not sure that's true, son—you already needed my help."

That stung. Wes stopped, dropped the golf bag, and reached inside to retrieve the blue neoprene cooler. He unzipped it and pulled out the thick stack of bills, now thawed and dripping with water. "Here... I didn't need it after all. And I'm good with The Carver."

Randolph hesitated, then took the money and gave it a shake. "Tell you what... I'll hang onto this. And if you decide you want to go to college, this money will pay for your first year. If, on the other hand, you decide you want to give professional poker a try, it'll go toward your first big tournament. Deal?"

Wes wavered. It was a great offer... so why did it feel like a trick? He chewed on his lip until it bled, then nodded. "Deal."

CHAPTER 15

"THANKS FOR THIS," Carlotta said to Coop. "The Wrens have taken up your entire day."

"No problem," Coop said, turning his car into the school parking lot to merge with the long line of vehicles collecting kids. "But next time I pick up Prissy, I'll drive the 'vette so she'll look cool."

"Oh, she'd love that." Carlotta wondered if he realized he'd said "next time."

She rather liked the sound of it.

"How do you think things went today with Mom's imaging? Be honest. Has Dr. Cullum indicated anything to you?"

"I would tell you if I knew something," Coop said, "but no, Dr. Cullum hasn't shared anything about the test results with me, nor would she. My advice is still to hope for the best until you have reason to think otherwise."

She nodded.

"Your mother seemed more calm today."

"That's because Randolph went with us this time—although I'm sure you noticed he spent every spare moment talking in the corner on his phone."

"He must be busy reestablishing their lives."

"*His* life," Carlotta corrected. "He's scarcely around."

"He's been helping Wes with repairs on the townhouse, hasn't he?"

"Some... but Wes says he's there for an hour or so, then leaves and doesn't say where's he going."

"So you haven't spent much time with Randolph one on one?"

She shook her head. "Although I agreed to go with him to an event at the club tomorrow evening."

"Getting introduced back into high society, huh?"

She laughed. "I suppose it will mean a lot to Randolph to be able to rub elbows with that group again, now that he's been vindicated."

"He deserves that, don't you think?"

Carlotta relented with a nod. "I just wish Mom could be there with him instead of me. She walks around in a fog worrying about him being with Liz behind her back—it's awful. If she's going to be stuck in a certain period in her mind, why does it have to be the most traumatic time of her life?"

"Unfortunately, that's how the brain works sometimes. The most traumatic events leave an indelible impression on our brains. Evolutionists would say it's to keep us from repeating mistakes." He smiled. "Of course, it can work opposite, too, meaning sometimes people keep reliving the bad thing in the hope that something will be different this time around."

"Meaning Valerie might be reliving finding out about Dad's affair with Liz in the hope that this time, it won't be true?"

"Possibly. Or that things will turn out differently this time."

Carlotta turned her head to look for Prissy... that described her habitual rebounding to Jack, reliving a situation in the hope things would turn out differently this time. But she was keeping her word to herself to keep her distance.

She looked back to Coop. "Did you finish the autopsy on the roller derby girl?"

He gave a curt nod. "Her larynx was crushed with the wooden crutch and she asphyxiated, just as it appeared at the crime scene."

"Any theories on who might've done it?"

"You'd have to talk to the lead detective about that," he said

105

lightly.

"No need. I'm sure the police have everything under control."

"Uh-huh."

She saw Prissy and waved. "There she is."

Prissy came running up to the car, and Coop climbed out to open the rear door for her. "Hi, Dr. Coop!"

"Hi, Prissy."

"Hi," Carlotta added.

"Hey," Prissy replied in a half-hearted voice.

Carlotta tried not to react to the diss. "How was your day?"

"This dress was itchy. I told you I didn't want to wear it, but you made me anyway."

"Because it was the third one you tried on, and we were going to be late."

"Whatever."

Push... pull... push.

Prissy leaned forward. "Can we go get ice cream, Dr. Coop?"

Coop looked to Carlotta. "I'll let you decide."

In other words, make her the heavy. "You don't want to ruin your appetite. Birch is making lasagna for dinner."

Prissy frowned and sat back. "How were Mommy's tests today?"

"She got through them very well, but we won't have the final results for a few days."

The little girl nodded, then looked out the window.

She was processing a lot, Carlotta realized. Dealing with new surroundings, new people, a new school, and all while watching her mother slip away. It had to be terrifying.

"I changed my mind," Carlotta said. "Let's get ice cream."

Prissy grinned. "Yea!"

Coop looked at Carlotta, then winked and nodded his approval.

He chatted with Prissy all the way to the ice cream shop, drawing her out and getting her to talk about school and friends she'd made. Her sister was more forthcoming with him than with her, she noticed. She hoped soon Prissy would soften toward her. At the moment, she seemed to be happy to resist Carlotta at every possible turn.

At the ice cream shop, she took her time choosing which flavor she wanted, getting a sample of several before she settled on a scoop of rainbow sherbet, and one scoop of strawberry. Carlotta chose a scoop of pistachio, and Coop got a mocha shake for easier driving. Prissy was animated on the short ride to the house, giggling at Coop's corny knock, knock jokes. They were all laughing when they pulled into the driveway.

Prissy looked out the window. "Jack!"

Sure enough, Jack's car was parked at the curb. He climbed out, holding a box.

"Were you expecting him?" Coop asked mildly.

"Not at all," she said, wondering what had prompted this visit.

By the time they alighted, Prissy was already out of the car and running toward him. He set the box on the ground, then lifted the lid. A little yellow head appeared.

"A puppy!" Prissy shouted.

"I hope it's okay," Jack said as she and Coop walked up. "I found him in a dumpster. I took him to a vet to have him checked out. He's had all his shots."

"Thank you, Jack! I love him so much," Prissy cried, pressing her nose up against the puppy's; who licked her until the little girl giggled uncontrollably. She offered what was left of her ice cream to the puppy, who gobbled it down to adorable face-staining effect.

"Yes, thank you, Jack," Carlotta murmured. "It was nice of you." But to Coop she mouthed, *I'm sorry*. She should've let him get Prissy a puppy when he'd first mentioned it. Now Jack would always be the hero in the little girl's eyes.

"It's fine," Coop whispered for her ears only. "As long as she's happy. But I'm going to take off. I need to drop by the morgue to check on some things."

She smiled. "Okay. I can't thank you enough for today."

He smiled back. "Any time."

"Soon," she said.

He nodded, then waved. "Bye, Prissy! See you, Jack."

"See you, Coop."

But Prissy was too distracted by the puppy to respond.

Carlotta waved as Coop drove off, and when his car went by her, she remembered something from the day she and Hannah had found Babs in her bedroom. She made her way over to Jack, who was leaning against his car, looking pleased with himself.

"I didn't mean to break up the party," he said.

"You didn't. Coop found a doctor who's running tests on Mom, and he's been going with us to help things along."

"I hope you get good news."

"Thank you. I'm trying to be optimistic." She noticed he was almost smiling watching Prissy and the puppy. "You're in a good mood."

"Hm? Ah, maybe so."

"What's the occasion?"

He shrugged. "Just an above-average day."

"Any leads on the roller derby girl's case?"

"Barbara Mayfield? No. The security cameras weren't working, and none of the neighbors heard anything."

"You think it was a robbery gone bad?"

He worked his mouth back and forth. "Could be."

"Or?"

"Or... it could've been staged to look like a robbery. Most thieves don't take the time to look through silverware drawers in the kitchen, but not touch a jewelry box in the bedroom."

"I noticed that, too," she offered. "And I just recalled something about the crime scene I didn't mention."

She had his attention. "What?"

"An odor I noticed when I walked in. I couldn't place it at the time, but when Coop drove by and I smelled the exhaust, I remembered—it smelled like car fumes or asphalt or something like that. Does that mean anything to you?"

"No."

"Do you have any suspects at all?"

"Not really."

"Hannah said she was divorced. What about the ex?"

"We looked at the ex, he lives in another state, couldn't have done it. A handful of neighbors have records for minor things, but no red flags went up when they were questioned."

"Current boyfriend?"

"We talked to most of her roller derby teammates. They said she doesn't have a boyfriend—or a girlfriend."

"So it could've been a woman?"

"Possibly, although even with a broken leg, the victim looked as if she could counter another woman who was overpowering her." He pursed his mouth. "Did you notice the broken crutch?"

Carlotta nodded. "At first I thought she'd used it to wedge the door closed, and it broke when the intruder came in."

"But?" he prompted.

"I, um, noticed a dark hair on the bottom of the rubber tip, so I'm guessing she used it to defend herself."

He gave her a flat smile. "We have the hair, running DNA on it now, but it'll take a while. Anything else, Sherlock?"

Carlotta started to say no, then a memory surfaced and she snapped her fingers. "Maybe." She opened in her purse. "While I was waiting outside, I leaned against the rail and got something on my hand." She found the tissue and opened it, revealing the black substance. A small ring of grease surrounded the smear. Carlotta sniffed it. "Petroleum—this is what I smelled when I walked inside the apartment."

Jack took the tissue, then lifted it to his nose. "Motor oil."

"Does it mean anything?"

"Not yet. I thought I told you not to touch anything."

"It wasn't intentional."

He refolded the tissue. "Thanks."

She blinked. "You're welcome. Have you considered the deaths of two people connected to the same roller derby team could be linked?"

"You mean, like a rival team knocked them off?" He gave a little laugh. "One was a drug overdose with hundreds of witnesses, and one was a murder in a bad part of town known for murders. Besides, why would someone on a rival team kill a mascot and a woman who's already out for the season?"

"I know… it just seems so coincidental."

"More like bad universal timing."

He looked at her in a way that made her feel as if that last comment was meant for them.

Then he pushed away from the car. "Time for me to go. Oh, by the way, Walt Tully has been deemed medically able to withstand incarceration. He's supposed to surrender himself into custody tomorrow."

She exhaled. "Then maybe Peter's case can be separated from the others, and he'll get bail."

Jack walked around to open the driver side door. "I'll be hoping for the best where your mother's concerned."

Carlotta smiled. "Thanks, Jack."

"Bye, Jack!" Prissy shouted. "Thanks for the puppy. You made me so, so happy!"

"Good. What are you going to name him?"

"I already named him," Prissy announced. "His name is Jack, of course!"

He laughed, then waved and swung into the car.

Carlotta gave a little wave, her tongue firmly tucked into her cheek. And now they had a pet named after him. Perfect. Just… perfect.

CHAPTER 16

"AN UPDATE ON the arrest of employees of local investment firm Mashburn & Tully, accused of bilking their clients hundreds of millions of dollars in a Ponzi and counterfeiting scheme," the radio announcer said.

Carlotta leaned forward. "Will you turn up the volume, please?" she asked the Uber driver.

The woman obliged.

"The sole partner not yet in custody, Walter Tully, was scheduled to surrender to the D.A.'s office for arrest this morning, but he failed to show. Tully's attorney, who did appear, said he has been unable to reach his client and has no idea of his whereabouts. Fulton County District Attorney Kelvin Lucas had this to say: 'At this point, Walter Tully is considered to be a fugitive from the law.'

Carlotta knew the man who had pursued her father—she'd endured his questioning and persecution on more than one occasion, and could tell from his voice he was livid.

'Walter Tully is charged with numerous federal crimes, and any person who aids and abets Mr. Tully will be charged as well. My office will not allow these crimes against so many victims who have lost their life savings to go unpunished.' If you have any information on the whereabouts of Walter Tully, you are advised to contact the police or the Fulton County D.A.'s office..."

She sat back, reeling over how the tables had turned. Walt

Tully had been Randolph's closest friend and her godfather, but when her parents had disappeared, he hadn't lifted a hand to help her and Wes, which was even more unconscionable considering how young they'd been at the time.

And how utterly ill-equipped and unprepared she'd been to deal with the situation.

Worse, Walt's daughter Tracey had been a classmate in the private school she attended and had made her life a living hell, sharing made-up accusations that Randolph and Valerie were in some exotic locale living it up with stolen money.

Teenagers could be vicious.

That was all behind her now, but it had left her scarred.

"We're here ma'am."

Carlotta startled to realize the car was sitting in front of the Bedford Manor Country Club.

Her door was opened by a valet, who welcomed her and offered her a gloved hand.

She pulled up the hem of her long blue Michael Kors gown enough to slide out of the car, then stood for a moment to take in the decadent surroundings. The club was ancient, traditional, and sprawling. New wings and floors had been added every few years to accommodate the explosion of the tony area of Buckhead and its membership rolls. The massive facility sat on a steep rise—the best possible vantage, she noted wryly, for its members to look down on everyone else. The white columns were illuminated with uplights, and its walkway twinkled with star-shaped lights to guide the privileged home.

She tipped the driver and the valet, and moved to make way for the line of cars behind her, each carrying decked-out guests.

At the entrance, suited men and gowned women exchanged greetings. She spotted Randolph, waiting for her as he'd promised. He was resplendent in a black tuxedo suit, smiling and glad-handing other members just as if he'd never left their ranks. He turned his head and spotted her, then lifted his hand and walked forward to meet her.

"You look lovely, sweetheart." He hugged her and kissed her on the cheek. She inhaled the spicy scent of his cologne, happy for this moment she couldn't have imagined only a few weeks ago.

"Thank you, Daddy."

"Did you hear the news about Walt?"

She nodded. "In the car, on the way over. Where do you think he is?"

He shook his head. "Who knows? Not far, I'd guess. Walt isn't built to live on the run, to be hunted."

The flicker of despair in his eyes as he flashed back to his life as a fugitive gave her a glimpse into how stressful it must have been for Randolph, to be constantly looking over his shoulder while keeping an eye on his sick wife and young child. She vowed to try to be more understanding of why he was so eager to get back to the life he'd been forced to abandon.

"That reporter friend of yours, Rainie Stephens—she's still pursuing me for an interview."

Carlotta laughed. "She's persistent, that's why she's good at her job. Have you given her an answer?"

"Not yet. Shall we go in? I'm dying to show off the most beautiful daughter a man could possibly have."

She beamed. "I've missed you *so* much."

"Same here," he said, patting her hand.

They walked into the club, and all eyes turned toward them—some looked guilty, some looked happy, some looked envious. She'd be lying if she said it didn't feel special to be on the arm of the man of the hour. Everyone was solicitous, eager to let bygones be bygones, which meant to simply ignore the fact that they'd ever accused Randolph of anything illicit.

They had known all along he couldn't possibly be guilty.

They had always suspected something wasn't quite right with the firm.

They had been so pleased to know they'd been right all along, about everything.

Carlotta nodded and smiled and shook hands and accepted awkward hugs from people who had shunned her before, when she had attended events as Peter's date. And now it was as if Peter didn't exist—no one asked about him, no one seemed to care that he'd fallen on his sword to try spare a few clients when he'd uncovered the awful truth. It was the way of this group, she realized, to sweep the ugly under the rug and only celebrate the sparkly things and pretty people.

When she started to feel overwhelmed, Carlotta excused herself and escaped to the women's lounge. The urge for a cigarette was strong, but she was determined to quit this time. She rummaged through her purse looking for a mint.

The door to the lounge opened, and Tracey Tully Lowenstein walked in a little unsteadily. She was harshly pretty and lavishly dressed.

"Well, well, if it isn't the celebrity daughter of Randolph Wren." Tracey had a drink in her hand and from the look of her, at least two in her stomach.

Carlotta schooled her face. "Hi, Tracey."

"Surprised to see me here?" she slurred.

"A little," Carlotta admitted.

"Why, because my daddy is on the lam?" She laughed. "Am I supposed to stay home because my father is a criminal?"

"No," Carlotta said carefully.

"Maybe you can give me some pointers on what to do when your father is a bad man."

She set her jaw. "Except my father isn't a bad man."

"Well, maybe he didn't steal that money, but he cut corners at the firm like everyone else. And everyone knows what a philanderer he was… is. Your poor, poor mother. Maybe it's better she's losing her mind."

Carlotta's hand shook from wanting to slap her. "I'm leaving now."

Tracey started to say something, then covered her mouth with her hand and ran for a stall. Carlotta exited on the sounds of her retching. The exchange had left her with a bad taste in her own mouth, but she tried to chalk it up to Tracey's drunkenness and the change in her family's fortune.

Karma was a bitch.

In her small bag, Carlotta's phone vibrated. She stopped in the quiet hallway outside the lounges and pulled it out, surprised to see Fulton County Correctional Center come up on the screen.

And what did it say that she had the county lockup as a contact in her phone?

She connected the call, and an automated voice came on the line. "Will you accept a call from inmate Peter Ashford? Please say yes or no."

"Yes," she said, gripping the phone tightly. After a series of clicks, Peter's voice sounded.

"Carly?"

"Hi, Peter. How are you?"

"Not so good," he said, sounding like a broken man. "My attorney just told me that Walt has disappeared."

"Yes, I heard that as well."

"Now the judge has determined we're all flight risks, so even if my case is separated from the others', my chances of getting out on bail seem nonexistent at this point."

She swallowed hard. "I'm sorry, Peter."

"So am I. I was hoping for one last bit of freedom before the trial and... whatever happens next."

"Hang in there, Peter. I'll come visit again soon."

"Carly," he said, sounding a little desperate. "Randolph..."

"What about Randolph?"

"He's not... what you think he is."

She frowned. "What's that supposed to mean?"

He made an anguished noise. "Nothing... forget I said anything. My mind is going all over the place, and so is my mouth. I'll let you go, Carly. Remember that I love you."

The call ended and Carlotta sat staring at the phone. Had Peter been talking out of his head?

Trying to set aside the gravity of his plight, Carlotta stowed her phone and rejoined the party.

It was a gala to benefit a series of charities—all good causes, and all good reasons for getting dressed up and eating and drinking too much. She threaded her way through the crowd, looking for her dad. Along the way, she returned smiles and nods from people she didn't know, but who apparently knew her.

When she spotted Randolph, he was talking to a lovely blonde. Something about their body language spoke of familiarity. And speaking of familiar, the woman could've been Liz Fischer's twin... the type of mistress Randolph was attracted to? As Carlotta walked closer, a knot formed in her stomach.

Please, don't be doing this again, Dad... not to mom while she's sick... not to us.

Her father's liaison with Liz had set so many terrible things in motion. Hadn't he learned his lesson?

"Hello," she said pleasantly, stepping between them.

They each took a self-conscious step back.

"Hi, Sweetheart," her father said, his voice a little too cheerful. Then he lifted his hand in a wave to the woman. "It was nice to talk to you."

"Um... same to you," the woman said woodenly, then she turned and strode away.

"Who was that?" Carlotta asked.

"Hm? Oh, just an acquaintance, the wife of someone or other. I don't even recall her name, else I would've introduced you."

Carlotta wondered if he could see the skepticism in her eyes.

He gave a little laugh and reached for her hand. "Let's dance, sweetheart. We haven't danced together in far too long."

She nodded and followed Randolph to the dance floor where he swept her into a waltz. She'd forgotten what a good dancer he was. Her mother, too—they had always been the stars of any ball.

"I wish Mom were here," Carlotta said, realizing when the words came out that she meant it in more ways than one.

Randolph's eyes dimmed, but he didn't respond, just pulled her closer.

Carlotta put her head on his shoulder so she didn't have to see the guilt on his face.

CHAPTER 17

WES STIRRED the risotto, tasted it, then replaced the lid. Carlotta would be impressed—although that wasn't difficult since his sister didn't cook. He'd taken over that job at the age of twelve, when he had tired of frozen pizza and boxed macaroni and cheese.

He glanced around the kitchen, gratified at least the holes in the walls had been repaired, if not painted. He'd spent the afternoon cleaning up drywall dust and straightening the kitchen enough to cook and eat in. He hoped Carlotta would be impressed with the progress enough to start planning her move back.

He was half afraid she wasn't going to... and he missed her, dammit.

He went to his room to change shirts and checked on Einstein—and the mouse. After so many days of being terrorized, it was catatonic, but still alive.

"One more day," he warned Einstein. "Then I'm going to have to force-feed you—and you know how much we both hate that."

Wes frowned. He'd tacked the number for the reptile rescue society on his bulletin board. Maybe Einstein needed a change of scenery for his own health. Or a mate.

He could relate. If he had to go to the rest of his life without sex, he might starve himself to death, too.

And although Meg hadn't exactly put the moves on him, she

was at least treating him as if he was human. He could work with that.

From his desk, his handheld poker video player buzzed twice, indicating it needed to be charged. Wes reached for the charging cable, then stopped. His father's offer—college or poker—still weighed heavily on his mind. The start of the fall semester wasn't far away, so he'd have to make a decision soon.

He'd played the handheld game so much, he'd worn the finish off the buttons.

Wes pressed his lips together, then opened a drawer and put the game out of sight.

At the sound of voices, he glanced out the window and fought back a smile. Carlotta had been waylaid by their favorite busybody neighbor, Mrs. Winningham. He went to rescue her.

When he opened the front door, Mrs. Winningham's annoying voice rode the air.

"… it's certainly been more quiet around here since you've been gone. No hearses and no police cars in and out of the driveway at all hours of the day." She stood talking over the tall fence she'd erected to keep the Wrens and their crabgrass out of her yard. She was holding her ugly dog Toofers, seemingly oblivious to his snarling. The dog hated his sister.

"That's good, Mrs. Winningham," Carlotta said, juggling a shopping bag.

"Hi, Sis," he called. "Glad you're here, I really need your help inside. The kitchen's on fire."

Carlotta knew he was kidding, but it was satisfying to see the alarm on Mrs. Winningham's face.

Carlotta jogged up the steps. "Bye, Mrs. Winningham."

The woman leaned over the fence. "Should I call the fire department?"

"No, we got it," Carlotta called, then stepped inside and closed the door. They both laughed.

"Phew," Carlotta said. "I don't miss that."

Wes felt a little pang… it didn't sound as if she was ready to come back at all.

She handed him the shopping bag. "I brought you some groceries and things."

"Thanks."

Carlotta put her hands on her hips and turned in the living room. "This place looks a lot better than the last time I was here."

He grinned. "You think so?"

"Sure." She peered into the hallway and opened the door to her room. "But a lot left to do, huh?"

His grin dissolved. "Yeah… but we're making headway. And I was thinking of suggesting to Dad that we hire painters and some other laborers to speed things along."

"But what's the hurry?"

"I thought you might be feeling crowded at the Buckhead house."

"Not really."

"Or you know, if things there are awkward."

She smiled. "No, everything there is… great."

"Oh," he said, his shoulders falling. "Good."

She inhaled deeply, then frowned. "Something's burning."

He rushed into the kitchen and cursed. The risotto had cooked down too quickly, and the bottom had scorched, badly. "Dammit," he muttered, pulling the pan off the burner.

Carlotta looked over his shoulder at the hardened mass that had set up like concrete. "What was it?"

"Mushroom risotto," he said miserably.

"Looks like I made it."

He frowned. "It's ruined."

"So… make something else. How about an omelet?"

He sighed and nodded. But he wasn't going to lure Carlotta back with scrambled eggs. He trudged to the refrigerator. "How was the party last night?"

"Great. Dad was the man of the hour."

"That's good."

"How has it been working with him?"

"Great," he said. "Really great."

She nodded. "And how's everything else? Any update on your charges?"

"Not yet. Still grooving my sporty ankle bracelet."

"And how's Meg?"

He couldn't keep from smiling. "Coming around."

"Yeah? Good."

"How are things with you and Coop?"

She shrugged. "Fine. He's such a terrific guy."

"So why don't you fall in love with him already?"

"It's not that simple. I don't want to mess things up. It's still so soon after Peter... and did you hear Jack gave Prissy a puppy?"

He frowned. "Brown-noser."

"She named it Jack."

"Shit."

"I know, right?"

He started cracking eggs into a bowl. "So what's the deal there?"

"Where?"

"With Jack?"

She shook her head. "No deal... he has other things on his plate."

"Does he ever mention Liz?"

"No, but I know he's in touch with her. Does Dad ever mention Liz?"

"Not really."

"Does he ever mention... anyone else?"

He frowned. "What do you mean?"

"Nothing. I brought a red pepper, do you want to add it to the omelet?"

"Sure." Wes prepared the omelets, watching Carlotta under his lashes. She seemed antsy, was she already wanting to leave?

From his bedroom came a loud thumping noise, following by thrashing.

"Einstein," he said. "Guess he finally decided to eat."

She grimaced. "Sorry, but I don't miss that snake either."

"I'm getting rid of him."

Her head came up. "What?"

"I'm giving him to a reptile rescue."

"But you love that snake."

He shrugged. "It's a boy's pet." He shoveled the omelets onto the two plates on the table, then they both sat down. "Besides... I want you to feel like you can come back."

Carlotta's hand stopped midway to her mouth.

"But only if you want," he said with a shrug.

She set down her fork. "Wes, are you trying to say something?"

He concentrated on pouring hot sauce on his eggs. "Just that I understand if you want to stay with them. I know it's much better there, and you want to be with them, and... Mom wants you there." As opposed to him.

Carlotta didn't say anything for a while. "Wes... things aren't good there."

His eyes widened. "What? But you seem so happy."

"I'm happy they're back, yes. I'm glad to know they're safe, and Prissy was a nice surprise." She sighed. "But it's so awkward and it feels like everyone is doing their own thing, but in the same house. I guess I just thought they would come back and everything would suddenly be good."

He nodded. "So did I. But you and Dad... you two are so much alike, and you get along so great. I remember it was always like that between you. I used to be jealous."

Carlotta smiled. "Dads and sons can be hard."

"He made me an offer."

"What kind of offer?"

"He wants to buy a driving range and me help run it."

"And how do you feel about that?"

"Honestly? It sounds awful."

She laughed. "So tell him."

"But if I do it, he says he'll back me to become a professional poker player."

Carlotta pursed her mouth. "Well, that's what you've always wanted... isn't it?"

"Yeah." He put a big wad of eggs into the mouth, chewed, and swallowed. "But lately I've also thought about going to college... med school, maybe. And keep working with Coop."

Her face lit up. "That sounds wonderful, Wes."

"Dad doesn't think I'm up to that, that I'm not disciplined enough."

Carlotta wiped her mouth with her napkin. "What do you think?"

He shrugged. "I am kind of a screw-up—you know that better than anyone."

"You've made mistakes—who hasn't? But this is your life, Wes. Make sure you choose what you want, and not just what Randolph wants for you."

He pushed his eggs around on the plate, wishing the answer would appear, like reading tea leaves.

Her cheeks puffed out with an exhale. "I wish this all could be easier, for all of us."

"My probation officer suggested a family counselor, said it might help with the transition."

"That's actually not a bad idea. I'll look into it. Meanwhile, I've been thinking we should have a family portrait taken."

He nodded. "That's a good idea."

She angled her head. "And for now, I think you need to keep Einstein around so you don't get lonely."

He grinned. "Okay."

"But don't get too used to having this place to yourself. I'll be back, and probably before you want me to."

Wes's heart bounced up. That couldn't happen.

She set down her fork. "Thanks for dinner—it was good, as always." She looked around the cramped kitchen. "Gosh, we've shared lot of meals in here, haven't we?"

"Yeah. And a lot of laughs."

"And some tough times," she said. "But we got through it, didn't we?"

He grinned. "We sure did."

Carlotta leaned over and gave him a hug and for once, he didn't resist. She was an amazing sister, and he owed her everything. "I love you," he whispered.

"I love you back," she said, hugging him tighter.

"Okay, okay," he said with a laugh, drawing back before he started bawling like a baby.

Carlotta stood up to clear her plate, then her gaze caught on the little Christmas tree and gifts, sitting just inside the living room, now covered with a layer of drywall dust. "We still need to open our gifts."

"Dad said we would when Mom is having a good day."

Her chest rose visibly as she inhaled. "We're supposed to get the test results Friday. Then hopefully we'll know how many good days are ahead."

CHAPTER 18

"ARE YOU SURE we won't get caught?" Carlotta asked, creeping into the empty Bruised Peaches locker room.

"Absolutely... not," Hannah said. "But if we do, I'm on roller skates, so I'll get away."

Carlotta gave her friend a wry smile. "How was practice?"

"Somber. Missy is inconsolable. She's our best jammer, but I think she's going to have to sit out Saturday's match."

"I'm sorry we're going to miss it," Carlotta said. "We're having a family portrait taken."

"Ah—nice. No big deal, we still have several matches left in the season. And hopefully Missy will bounce back from this."

"Was Missy one of the co-founders of the group, too?"

"No, she's actually pretty new to roller derby, has only been competing for about a year. But she and Babs bonded, I think, over their failed marriages."

Carlotta made a rueful noise. She had an inkling of how Missy must feel—if she lost Hannah to the hands of a low-life murderer, she'd be inconsolable, too.

"Why are you looking at me like that?" Hannah asked.

"Like what?"

"Like you wanna kiss me or something. Haven't you done the deed with Coop yet?'

"No."

"Yeah, well, you need to. And when you do, make a video, will you?"

Carlotta rolled her eyes. "Let's do this and get out of here. Which locker belonged to Babs?"

"The one on the end, with the black ribbon."

Someone had tied a big black bow on the handle of the locker, and skaters had written tributes in marker on the door.

We love you, Babs!

Keep rolling on the other side!

This season is for you!

"There's a padlock on it," Carlotta said.

Hannah unzipped her gym bag and removed a huge pair of bolt cutters. "Why do you think I brought these?"

"Now I know what happened to Chance's balls."

"Stand back."

Carlotta stepped back and watched Hannah cut through the steel lock in one snap of her elbows.

"That's great, but now isn't everyone going to know someone was in her locker?"

From her bag o' tricks, Hannah pulled a new lock. "Ta-da!"

"But if we find something, I call Jack, deal?"

"Deal. And if not, we put on the new lock, and no one's the wiser."

Hannah opened the locker. Inside were pictures of the team, a mirror, makeup bag, skate keys, protein bars, a first aid kit, hair brushes and ties and a bunch of miscellaneous junk—nothing of particular interest until they got down to a spiral bound notebook.

Carlotta's heartrate picked up as she opened it, then sank when she realized it wasn't a diary, but hand-written stats from the matches, with notes Babs had written to herself in the margins. "She was serious about roller derby," Carlotta murmured.

"It's a culture. And just the short time I've been in it, I see the positive things it does for a woman's self-esteem. Not all women have the confidence to move bodies from crime scenes, or track down murderers… or, in your case, find your mother."

Carlota looked up. "Thanks for that. It sounds like the derby is empowering."

"Yeah. For some of these girls, being in the roller derby gives them the courage to speak up for themselves and make positive changes in their lives." Hannah gestured to the locker. "So did we strike out?"

"Looks like it, although we really weren't expecting to find anything." Carlotta sighed. "Maybe Babs left her door unlocked because she was dealing with her crutches and her hands were full and some passing by tweaker came in looking for quick cash and freaked out when he realized she was home." She closed the notebook to put it back. "Maybe this was just one of those times when a series of unfortunate events led to something tragic."

A slip of colored paper fell from the notebook—a sticky note, sans the sticky, so it probably wasn't recent. Carlotta picked it up.

Don't text anymore, too risky. M

"M." She showed the note to Hannah. "Missy?"

"Probably, considering how close they were."

"So who would Missy have been afraid would see texts from Babs? Her husband?"

Hannah pursed her mouth. "Maybe. Missy went through a divorce a few months ago."

"Do you think she and Babs were having an affair?"

"No," Hannah said flatly. "That's a stereotype—people think because these girls are strong and assertive, that they're lesbians. But most of them are heterosexual women with husbands and kids, like me." She snorted. "Well, okay my husband *is* a kid, but you get my drift. Babs told me straight up she'd shout it to the world if she were gay or bi, but she wasn't. Same for Missy. They both just happened to marry shitty guys."

Carlotta squinted. "You said they bonded over their bad marriages."

"Yeah."

"So... I wonder if Missy's husband blames Babs for the breakup?"

Hannah shrugged. "Could be."

"Do you know anything about him?"

"No, just that Missy still used her married name—Fuller—because she kept talking about how she wanted to go back to her maiden name."

Carlotta heard a noise outside the locker room. *"Shh—someone's coming."*

Someone humming and heading their way wearing hard-soled shoes—a security guard?

"Hide!" Hannah said. "I can be in here, but you can't."

While Hannah stuffed everything back into the locker, Carlotta looked for a place to take cover. Along the wall were barges of bottled water. She ducked into the small opening between them and the wall, and knelt down.

Most of the boxes contained plain water, but the cases stacked in front of her were the Tannenbaum's All Natural Energy Drink. She assumed this stash was supplied by the sponsor for the team's consumption. Each case was wrapped with a band specifying the date/match it was for, which made sense considering the label clearly stated the preservative-free drinks were perishable. Carlotta noticed the case earmarked for the upcoming Saturday game had been torn open and a bottle was missing. Someone was stealing product.

Had Lewis Bunning lifted a bottle while he was hiding out hoping for a peek of lingerie? Maybe he'd unwittingly spiked his drink with the poisonous SPICE while crouching in this very spot. The thought gave her a chill. She reached into the plastic to remove a bottle, studying the ingredients. She really needed to get more serious about what she put into her body. She shook the bottle and watched the herbs and bits of fruit fly around like a nutritious snow globe. Maybe she should take one—no one would miss it.

She overheard Hannah explaining to someone—a female—that she'd come back after practice to retrieve an item she'd left in her locker. The woman told her in a friendly, but firm voice that she couldn't be here after hours and needed to leave.

"No problem," Hannah said cheerfully. "I'm just going to pee before I jump into traffic, then I'll be on my way. Thanks!"

When the receding footsteps faded, Hannah whispered, "Come on, we gotta go."

Carlotta shoved the bottle back into the case, then emerged from her hiding place. Hannah yanked up the bag containing the bolt cutter and the sacrificed lock, and skated to the entrance of the locker room. After looking both ways, she signaled Carlotta to follow her. Carlotta jogged to keep up with her skating friend as they darted across the empty gymnasium floor and through a set of double doors into the parking lot.

"Phew," Hannah said. "That was close. I'd hate to get booted off the team for ransacking lockers. Do you need a ride home?"

Carlotta held up her new phone. "I just called a Lyft, thanks anyway."

"Okay." Hannah grinned. "Maybe I'll stop and visit my husband on the way home. Hey—good luck tomorrow." She held up two sets of crossed fingers.

Carlotta smiled. "Thanks." Her driver was pulling up just as Hannah was pulling away. On her ride home, she phoned Jack.

"Hi, Carlotta… do I want to know what you're into tonight?"

"Probably not," she admitted, thinking about the severed padlock. "But I do have something for you to follow up on in the Barbara Mayfield case."

"Oh, you're letting *me* follow up on a lead in a murder case? Thanks."

She frowned. "Do you want the info or not?"

"Lay it on me."

"When you interviewed her teammates, did you talk to a woman named Missy Fuller?"

"Missy Fuller... yeah, she was really upset, said they had been good friends. Best friends, I believe she said."

"Look into her ex-husband. There's a theory going around that he might have blamed the divorce on Babs."

"A theory going around, huh?"

"Yep."

"Okay, I'll run it up the flagpole." He made a thoughtful noise. "Any news on your mother's test results?"

"We're meeting with the doctors tomorrow."

"I'll be thinking about you," he said, his voice suddenly serious.

She closed her eyes briefly. "Thanks, Jack."

"How's the puppy?"

"Pissing on everything in sight." Not unlike his namesake. "Bye, Jack," she said, then ended the call.

CHAPTER 19

COOP REACHED over and wrapped his warm hand around Carlotta's jumpy one. "Try to relax," he whispered, then gave her hand a squeeze.

She nodded because she didn't trust her voice. All signs were pointing to a bad place. She, Coop, Randolph, and Wesley were huddled around the table in the cheery "bad news" room waiting for Dr. Cullum to give them the test results and, she hoped, a diagnosis. Coop had joined them under protest—she'd insisted they needed him to hear the doctor's pronouncement in case they misheard details and needed clarification later. Because she was relatively sure if the doctor started using words like "irreversible" and "progressive decline," she was going to shut down.

On the other side of her, Wesley seemed more composed, although under the table she could see his leg was jumping. Still he shot her a hopeful smile.

On the other side of Wes, Randolph's face was uncharacteristically stoic, as if he'd already resigned himself to the worst, and this meeting was simply a confirmation.

In another room across the hall, Birch sat with Valerie, who was undoubtedly unaware her fate was being discussed elsewhere.

The door opened and Carlotta's vitals ratcheted higher when Dr. Cullum walked in, along with two other physicians they'd never met.

Any news that required a tag team to deliver it couldn't be

good.

Dr. Cullum introduced her colleagues, but their names ran together in Carlotta's mind. The doctors launched into the types of tests they'd run and how the results had been verified.

Wesley sat forward. "Look, can we just cut to the chase, here? What's wrong with my mom?"

Carlotta had never been more proud of him.

Dr. Cullum nodded. "You're right—let's get to it." She smiled. "I have good news. In fact, in our line of work, this is about as good as it gets."

The other doctors nodded agreement.

"Mrs. Wren has a condition known as 'normal pressure hydrocephalus,' or NPH. It's a buildup of fluid in the cavities of the brain, which causes swelling and pressure on the areas that control memory, mobility and speech. NPH mimics many symptoms of classic dementia diseases."

"It still sounds very serious," Randolph said.

Like her father, Carlotta wasn't ready to celebrate.

"It is serious," Dr. Cullum assured him, "but it's treatable, and in most cases, the results are very good."

"You're saying her condition is reversible?" Carlotta asked.

"We can't make promises, of course, but with the placement of a shunt to drain the fluid and rehabilitation, it's possible your mother could regain most if not all the cognitive abilities she's lost."

Carlotta covered her mouth with her hand and inhaled through her fingers. She turned to Wes and they hugged.

Randolph, however, seemed flustered. "So the other doctors who saw my wife were just plain wrong?"

"NPH is rare," Dr. Cullum said. "Even some neurologists have never heard of it, or have never seen a case, and don't know what to screen for. Misdiagnosis is common."

"What causes NPH?" Wes asked, and Carlotta smiled to herself. She could see him someday sitting on the other side of this table.

One of the other doctors leaned in. "Cerebral spinal fluid malfunctions aren't completely abnormal, but when they happen, the brain has the ability to absorb or drain the excess fluid. When that ability is impaired, the cavities of the brain fill, causing NPH."

"But what causes that ability to be impaired?" Wes pressed.

"It can be another neurological event, such as a stroke. But for someone as young as your mother, my best guess would be a head injury."

Randolph shook his head. "I don't recall Valerie having a head injury."

"We're only speculating," the doctor said. "It could even be something from childhood, such as a case of meningitis."

"So what's the next step?" Coop asked.

"We'd like to start Mrs. Wren on medications today to diminish the pressure, and schedule surgery in a couple of weeks to insert a shunt."

"So we can take her home?" Carlotta asked.

Dr. Cullum nodded. "Yes. I'd like to see her in another week. But I think you'll begin to see improvements in her cognitive ability within a few days." She pushed to her feet, and her colleagues followed suit.

"Thank you very much," Randolph said, still looking shell shocked.

"Thank Dr. Craft—if he hadn't suspected a misdiagnosis and insisted I take on this case, Mrs. Wren and all of you might be facing a very different future."

Carlotta felt her jaw loosen. She turned to look at Coop, and he gave her a wink. Wonder infused her chest. "You knew?"

"Suspected," he said.

"Dr. Craft is in a unique position at the morgue to examine brains post-mortem and see firsthand how often dementia is misdiagnosed." Dr. Cullum smiled at him. "Well done, Doctor."

The two other physicians acknowledged him as well, extending handshakes as they left the room.

When the room door closed, Carlotta exhaled a breath she'd been holding since leaving Vegas. Wes grinned at Coop and high-fived him. "Dude—you're a superhero."

Randolph pushed to his feet to shake Coop's hand, but warning bells sounded in Carlotta's head... something about her father's reaction seemed off. It was as if he wasn't entirely happy about Valerie's prognosis. A terrible thought entered her head—had her father already written off Valerie? Had he been planning to have a life separate from his sick wife at home?

Her phone vibrated and she glanced at the screen, surprised to see Jack's name come up. She moved to the far corner of the room and connected the call.

"Hi, Jack. What's up?"

"Just thought you should know, Missy Fuller's husband has been arrested for murder of Barbara Mayfield. You were right—he blamed her for the divorce."

Her relief at being right was mitigated by the fact that the crime had still occurred. "So the hair on the crutch is his?"

"We won't have the DNA results on the hair for a while. But get this—Doug Fuller works at an instant oil change place."

"So the oil on the hand rail—"

"Will hopefully match the oil we found on the steering wheel of his truck. He's our guy, and I think we have the proof to put him away. Thanks, this was a win."

She smiled into the phone. "I'm glad."

"Have you talked to the doctors yet?"

"Yes," she said. "It's a win here, too."

"Ah, that's great news," he said. "Really, Carlotta, I'm happy for you... for all of you."

She turned and made eye contact with Coop. "Gotta go, Jack. Thanks for the update."

"Sure thing. Talk soo—"

But she'd already ended the call.

She stowed her phone then walked over to Coop. When Wes

and her dad headed toward the door, she said they'd be right out. Wes gave her a knowing look, then closed the door.

"What did Jack want?" Coop asked, reaching forward to lift a lock of her dark hair.

"I can't remember," she said, looping her arms around his neck. She looked into his intelligent, kind brown eyes. "You wonderful man... how can I ever thank you for what you've done?"

He grinned. "Are you open to suggestions?"

She nodded, then lifted onto her toes to kiss him. It wasn't their first kiss... but it was their best to-date. She slanted her lips over his and what started as a tender exploration quickly morphed into a more urgent need. He groaned into her mouth, and she opened wider to accept his tongue.

From the door, a cough sounded.

They parted to see Wes standing there. He jerked his thumb over his shoulder. "Uh, Coop there's a doctor out here who'd like to talk to you."

Coop nodded. "Sure, coming." He looked back to her, his eyes still shining with desire.

"I'm right behind you," she said with a smile. When he left, Carlotta sagged against the wall and touched her lips. "Wow," she whispered.

What was *that*?

CHAPTER 20

CARLOTTA'S SMILE was frozen.

"Prissy," Birch said, looking through the camera sitting on a tripod, "stop wriggling."

"I'm itching," Prissy whined. "It's this stupid, ugly sweater Carlotta made me wear."

Carlotta tried to maintain her smile. Maybe it had been a mistake to suggest she, Prissy, and their mother wear matching sweaters. It had seemed like such a good idea at the time, so... togethery.

"If I have to wear a stupid tie," Wes grumbled, "you have to wear a stupid sweater."

"At least you don't have to wear makeup," Randolph groused.

"It's powder for shine control," Birch said. "Your tan is throwing off the lighting for the whole picture."

"I'm hot," Prissy said, sagging.

"Jack, stay," Birch said to the puppy in front, on the floor. But the pet hadn't yet learned how to control its bladder, much less its impulse to run. It loped over to Birch, barking happily.

"I'll hold him," Prissy said. She scrambled to catch the puppy, then returned to her spot between Randolph and Wes.

"Okay, here we go," Birch said. "Smile, Valerie."

Valerie's head pivoted to look at everyone standing and sitting around her. "Who are all these people?"

"Uh-oh," Prissy said. "Jack had an accident. Guess he didn't like my sweater either."

Birch pinched the bridge of his nose. "Maybe we should take a break."

They all fell out, moving away from the stiff couch in the living room where they'd been sitting, leaning, or standing behind.

Carlotta looked at Wes. "Maybe this wasn't such a good idea after all."

He gave her a lopsided smile. "It might take a while to get it right, but we'll get it."

She hoped so. Suddenly it seem very important to get a portrait taken of their family... before it fell apart. Randolph had walked to the other end of the room, as far away from everyone as he could get. Something was clearly on his mind.

Wes had noticed, too, and his expression mirrored how she felt—wary. "Let's get something to drink," he suggested.

She followed him into the kitchen and pulled at the neck of her sweater. "It is kind of itchy," she admitted. "And kind of ugly."

He laughed and handed her a soda from the fridge. "Let's get this over with and we can catch the last of the roller derby match. Did you know Chance is the new team mascot?"

"Really?" She winced. "Not sure I want to see Chance in a unitard."

Wes laughed. "Yeah, no kidding. But he'd do anything for Hannah."

"They do seem to be making this marriage thing work." She tried to keep her tone casual. "Will Meg be at the derby tonight?"

A flush climbed his face. "Maybe."

"Then you should definitely wear the coat and tie."

He pursed his mouth and held out the tie. "You think?"

"You'll knock her socks off." She cracked open the soda and took a drink. "It should be a big crowd. Hannah said the team is doing a tribute to Babs tonight."

"Speaking of which..." Wes pointed to the television on the counter behind her.

She turned to see a news report with the caption "Man Arrested for Killing Roller Derby Star." A photo of Babs came on the screen—she was wearing the Bruised Peaches uniform and glammed up for the camera, her hair almost white, her expression tough and defiant. The picture switched to a dark-haired man being led away in handcuffs. Since Doug Fuller was wearing blue coveralls, she assumed he'd been taken into custody at his workplace.

She reached over to turn up the volume.

"A Marietta man named Douglas Fuller was arrested for the murder of his ex-wife's best friend, Barbara Mayfield. The two women skated together on the Bruised Peaches roller derby team. Police say Fuller accused Mayfield of encouraging his wife to divorce him. Fuller has previous domestic abuse charges. Mayfield's team is dedicating tonight's match to her memory."

Fuller kept his head bowed until he came close to the camera, then he looked up and mouthed something, a sneer on his face. When the police put him in the cruiser, he refused to duck. His bill cap was knocked off in the short struggle, which he lost.

"Looks like an angry dude," Wes remarked.

Carlotta squinted. "Can you back that up?"

"It's digital—sure." Wes picked up the remote control and rewound the clip.

"Can you slow down the part where he's saying something to the camera?"

"Yep."

"Can you make out what he's saying?"

Wes studied the screen as it moved frame by frame. "Those... bitches... will... get... theirs. Wow, sounds like this guy has it out for the entire team."

Carlotta nodded. The man's face was a frightening mask of pure hate. "Pause there."

Wes froze the picture.

"Look at his hat," she said.

Wes squinted. "What's on it?"

"The logo for the energy drink that sponsors the Bruised Peaches—Tannenbaum, I think."

"So?"

"So it just seems strange—if he hates the roller derby team, why would he be wearing one of the sponsor's hats?"

He shrugged. "Cause it was a freebie?"

Her mind raced. "Wes... if you wanted to hurt a group of people without actually being there, how would you do it?"

"Hypothetically, I guess maybe plant a bomb, or maybe poison the food they were going to eat."

"Or something they were going to drink?"

"Yeah, sure."

Her mind raced over recent images and conversations... the energy drink in Lewis Bunning's hand... the missing bottle from the case designated for the team to drink at tonight's match... Hannah's assertion the team was allowed to consume the energy drinks only at half-time.

Her throat convulsed at the implication. "Wes, when is half time for tonight's match?"

He glanced at the clock. "Assuming the match started on time, I'd say in a few minutes."

"Call Chance and tell him the energy drinks in the locker room are poisoned."

"Huh?"

"Just do it."

He unclipped his phone and started punching.

Carlotta grabbed her phone and called Jack. "Answer," she muttered as it rang. "Come on, Jack, answer."

"Hi, Carlotta," Jack said. "Make this quick, I'm on my way out the door."

"I think Doug Fuller poisoned energy drinks for the roller

derby team with the SPICE that killed the mascot."

"What? Okay, I changed my mind—slow down."

She rolled her eyes. "Do you know if Doug Fuller ever worked for a delivery company or drove a truck?"

"Yeah, he did. We went there first to question him, but he was fired a week ago and we chased him down at the oil change place. Here it is... Atlanta Wholesale Beverage Distributors."

Her heart thudded in her chest. She'd bet on her life the company distributed Tannenbaum All Natural Energy Drink—or rather, she'd bet on Hannah's life. "Fuller planted poisoned energy drinks for the team to consume at half-time. Call Coop and send a half-dozen ambulances to the gymnasium where the roller derby match is being played." She rattled off the address.

"Carlotta... that's a shitload of resources. If you're wrong, my captain will have my ass."

"But what if I'm right?"

He was quiet.

"Jack?"

"I'll make the calls... and I'm sure I'll see you there."

She ended the call, arching her eyebrows at Wes. "Did you talk to Chance?"

He shook his head. "No answer. I left a message."

"Keep calling," she said, yanking up her purse. "Let's go!"

They ran through the living room where Birch was fussing with the camera. "Let's try again to get this picture." Then he threw up his hands. "Where are you two going?"

"Hannah's in trouble," Carlotta said, then stopped. "Birch, how fast can you drive?"

He smiled and held out his hand for the keys.

Birch got them to the gymnasium in record time, just as ambulances were pulling in. When they ran inside, Carlotta glanced at the match clock and her heart nearly stopped. It was ten minutes into the half. But to her relief, the Bruised Peaches came rolling out of the locker room holding a banner with Babs' name and number on it. All ten of the skaters were cheering and shouting, Hannah the loudest. Chance was the exuberant new mascot, doing jumping jacks in his peach-colored unitard, his green wig bouncing along with this belly.

Jack came jogging up behind Carlotta. "Is that the team that was poisoned? They look fine to me."

"Which means we caught them before they drank it," she said. "That's a good thing."

"Uh-huh," Jack said with a frown. "I think I've listened to you one too many times."

Coop walked in and came up to stand next to them.

"False alarm," Jack said.

"But not a wasted trip," Coop said, winking at Carlotta. She smiled back.

"Ladies and gentlemen," the announcer said, "the Bruised Peaches have a half-time tribute to one of the founding members of the team who tragically lost her life earlier this week, Barbara Babs Mayfield."

The team lined up, holding the colorful banner in front of them. Missy Fuller, the team's jammer, took the microphone. She'd gotten three words into the tribute when the first skater dropped to the floor.

"Oh, no," Carlotta murmured.

At first, everyone was confused. Her teammates tried to help her up, then one of them collapsed as well… then another.

"Get the paramedics," Coop said to Jack.

Carlotta ran straight for Hannah. Her friend was standing in the melee, uncharacteristically still. When she saw Carlotta, she gave her woozy smile, then collapsed just as Carlotta reached her.

"Hannah!" Carlotta screamed. Her friend's face was as pale as the Goth makeup she sometimes wore, and she was deathly still.

"Hannah!" Chance ran and dropped to his knees beside her. "What's going on?"

A swarm of paramedics descended. Carlotta pulled Chance

away and through streaming tears, told him what happened. They stood back while paramedics pumped the stomachs of nine skaters, including Hannah. Only Missy Fuller remained standing, apparently the only one who hadn't consumed the energy drink... because her hateful ex-husband had once worked for the sponsor? She seemed confused and horrified, huddling with her coach.

The stomach pumping was hard to watch, but all was forgotten as each skater was revived, one by one.

Carlotta and Chance stood holding on to each other until Hannah's body heaved and she opened her eyes. Chance sobbed in relief, hanging onto Carlotta. She waved Wes over to hand him off, then followed Hannah as she was being transported to an ambulance.

Hannah's eyes fluttered open. "Hey... what happened?"

"Someone tried to poison the derby girls," Carlotta said. "But you're all too strong for that."

"Fuck yeah," Hannah said with a weak smile. Then she frowned. "What's with the ugly sweater?"

Carlotta released an immense sigh of relief... all was well.

CHAPTER 21

"LOOK AT THE DUCKS," Valerie said, pointing to the birds floating on the pond.

"Very pretty," Carlotta agreed. They were spending the afternoon at Piedmont Park. It was a beautiful spring day and Prissy had the day off school. She had brought her bike and the puppy, of course. Jack chased her as she zipped up and down the section of the paved path in front of the bench where Carlotta and Valerie sat.

"Stay where I can see you, Prissy," Carlotta called.

"And the turtles," Valerie added. "They're so funny."

Carlotta marveled over the difference in her mother after only a few days on the medication. Her mood had improved tremendously. She was less fixated on where Randolph was, and more engaged with everything around her. She was stronger and her mobility was better. And the light was beginning to return to her brown eyes.

"Do you remember coming here when you were little?" Valerie asked.

Carlotta blinked. "You brought me here when I was little?"

Valerie smiled. "Of course I did, Carlotta... you and Wesley, too. We came to the park for picnics all the time."

She nodded as her own memories were teased. "Yes... I do remember. We brought peanut butter and jelly sandwiches."

"Yes, strawberry for you, and grape for Wesley. And he always brought his kite."

"Yes… it was red, wasn't it?"

"That's right, with a long tail. He would run and run and run. Always running, that boy." Her face glowed with love.

Carlotta didn't push, had learned to let Valerie talk about whatever came to her mind. She would grab on to little pieces of memory and sometimes could spin them into full-blown days. It was as if her brain was awakening after a long sleep.

"Your father and I came here all the time when we were first married."

"Did you?"

"That's when we were poor," she said with a laugh. "And when your father was still in love with me."

"Dad is still in love with you, Mom."

She shook her head. "Your dad isn't around."

"I know he's gone a lot," Carlotta said. "But Randolph always comes home."

Valerie nodded, not entirely happy, but at least she didn't descend into one of her spells of demanding to see Randolph.

Carlotta looked up, and frowned when she didn't see Prissy. Despite what Carlotta had said, she'd ridden around the corner, out of sight. Or more likely she'd done it *because* of what Carlotta had said. The girl had to push every boundary.

"Prissy," she called. "Come back please where I can see you."

"She's a smart girl," Valerie said.

"I know… sometimes she's too smart for her own good."

Her mother laughed. "That's what I used to say about you."

"Prissy," Carlotta called louder. "I need for you to come back, please, right now."

When she didn't, Carlotta had a blip of panic, but told herself the girl was just being bratty today, or had found something interesting to look at. She stood and walked as far away from Valerie as she dared to look for Prissy, shouting her name, then came back.

"Mom, do you feel like walking?" she said, trying to keep her voice calm.

"As long as we don't go too fast."

"Okay, but try to hurry just a little."

"Are we late? I don't want to be too late because Randolph said he would be home for dinner. He works so hard at the firm."

She had backslid, Carlotta noted, but she didn't have time to be concerned. "Yes, Mom, we're late, so please try to walk as fast as you can."

"Prissy!" she shouted, pulling Valerie along the path. "Prissy, answer me!"

After what seemed like forever, they rounded the corner where Prissy had ridden. The path stretched long and empty before them, and wide open grassy fields spanned both sides. A few people walked or played around the path, but Prissy was nowhere in sight. She cupped her hands and shouted her sister's name until she was hoarse, urging Valerie along. She asked everyone she encountered if they'd seen a dark-haired little girl, but no one recalled. By the time they got to the end of the path, thirty minutes had gone by, and Carlotta was near full-fledge panic. Everyone knew perverts and predators hung out in parks to scoop up children. The only thing that kept her calm was thinking that a little girl, a bike, and a puppy would be a difficult package to abscond with. But when she saw Prissy's bike on the side of the path, abandoned, one wheel up in the air, her knees buckled.

"My daughter Carlotta has a bike like that," Valerie offered.

Carlotta scanned the area. A road that cut through the park was only fifty yards away. Someone could have pulled up, engaged Prissy in a conversation, then snatched her and driven off. By now they could be on Interstate 75 heading to Florida.

"Why are you crying?" Valerie asked.

"I can't find my little girl," Carlotta said, digging for her phone.

Valerie made a mournful noise. "Sometimes you can't be with your children. It's the hardest thing a mother has to bear."

Carlotta fumbled with the new phone, then saw she had four

missed calls from Jack… thinking it couldn't be a coincidence, she punched in his number. Terrible scenarios flew through her head… Jack was calling to break bad news…

"Carlotta?"

She choked out a sob. "Prissy is missing. Oh, God, Jack, I lost her."

"No, she's here, with me."

She inhaled sharply. "What? How?"

"Breathe. She's fine. She went looking for her puppy and got lost. Tell me where you are. I'll bring her to you."

She gave him the landmarks and he told her to sit tight. Valerie dried her tears of abject relief, unaware of why Carlotta was crying, but eager to soothe. It was one time Carlotta was glad her mother didn't fully understand what was going on. But it also gave her a glimpse into what it must have been like to be away from her children and not know if they were well. Valerie must have endured many sleepless night.

A few minutes later, Jack's sedan pulled up next to the curb. He got out and opened the back door and Prissy sprang out, holding the puppy. She seemed hesitant, and Carlotta realized she thought she was in trouble. So Carlotta bent over and opened her arms, and Prissy ran into them.

She hugged the little girl close, both of them crying.

"I'm sorry," Prissy kept saying. "I'm sorry, Carlotta."

"It's okay," she breathed. "Just promise me you'll never do that again."

"I promise."

She straightened and looked at Jack, who had walked down. "How did she wind up with you?"

She saw a city ambassador on the street and asked her to call me.

"I didn't have your phone number," Prissy said to Carlotta.

"It's okay. That's my fault. Stay with Mom, I'll be right back." She nodded to Jack and they walked back to his sedan.

"Thank you, Jack."

"Actually, I kind of feel like it's my fault for giving her the puppy."

"Don't feel like that. She loves it."

"Besides, I owe you one for the other night," he said. "If you hadn't put two and two and two together, nine women would be dead, including Hannah. That was impressive."

She inclined her head, accepting his rare praise.

"How is Hannah, by the way?"

"Fine," she said. "Wearing the whole incident like a badge of honor. Did you get a confession out of Fuller?"

He nodded, then shook his head. "It was one of the worst things I've ever seen. He was proud of what he did, said he only wished he'd been successful. He said he was justified to torment his ex-wife for choosing the roller derby over him."

"Hate is a powerful thing."

"So is love," he said, surprising her.

He nodded to her mother and sister. She looked back to see Valerie spinning in circles, holding Prissy by the hands and swinging her round and round. Prissy was screaming with pure joy. It was a beautiful sight, and Carlotta was struck with a sense of déjà vu. With astonishment, she realized Valerie used to swing her around like that on their trips to the park. She had forgotten that memory until this moment.

"I'll let you go," Jack said, then waved and turned toward his car.

Carlotta walked back to Valerie and Prissy, feeling full. They were lying in the grass looking up at the sky. She stretched out on the other side of Prissy, then closed her eyes and reveled in the warmth of the sun and the tickle of the breeze. Soon they could hear their mother's soft snores.

A few minutes later, Prissy reached over to clasp her hand.

Carlotta squeezed her small fingers.

"I need to tell you something," Prissy whispered.

Carlotta moved her head closer. "I'm listening," she whispered back.

"Mommy fell and hit her head hard just before she started forgetting things."

Carlotta turned her head to look at her little sister's tortured face. "What happened?"

"She tripped on one of my toys and hit her head on a table... really hard."

"And you didn't say anything?"

She shook her head. "She made me promise not to tell. She said Daddy would think she was drinking again." Then her eyes filled up with tears. "And I didn't want Daddy to know it was my fault." She was crying now. "It's my fault Mommy is sick."

"Shhh," Carlotta said, pulling her into a hug. "It's not your fault, it's no one's fault. People trip and fall all the time. And she's getting better now, so promise me you won't think about it anymore."

Prissy sniffled. "Okay."

"Promise?"

"I promise."

"Good." Carlotta smiled, then whispered, "I love you."

Prissy got a tense look on her face, then looked back to the sky. The little girl was so used to keeping her emotions bottled up.

"Do you love me back?" Carlotta asked softly.

Prissy breathed in and out, struggling. Then she said, "That's a rhetorical question."

Carlotta smiled, remembering her own words. *It makes so much sense, it doesn't require an answer.*

CHAPTER 22

WES WAS UNLOCKING his bike from the front of the city building, trying to ignore his shaking hands and the headache that had landed between his eyes like an axe. The Oxy was calling him today, and he suspected it had something to do with the decision he needed to make soon.

"I saw you at the roller derby Saturday night."

He turned his aching head to see Meg walking up, and instantly felt a little better. "Yeah?"

"Before they cleared everyone out."

Wes stabbed at his glasses. "Yeah, that was intense, wasn't it?"

"You were wearing a coat and tie."

"We were in the middle of shooting a family portrait when my sister put it all together about the poison, and we got there just in time."

"Your sister is an interesting person."

He nodded. "Carlotta is… the best. She thinks I'm the smart one, but she doesn't give herself enough credit. And she's always been there for me. I don't know what I'd do without her."

Meg gave him a little smile. "That's how I felt about my brother Tom."

Ugh. Here he was waxing poetic about siblings, and she'd lost her brother to an overdose. "I'm sorry, I didn't mean to make you sad."

"It's okay," she said. "I like to talk about Tom. I hope to tell you all about him someday."

He saw an opening. "Want to hang out tonight?"

"I... can't," she said. "I have to meet with my guidance counselor at Tech."

"Ah. You thinking about changing majors or something?"

She shook her head. "I'm leaving for Germany... tomorrow."

Shit. "Cool. When are you coming back?"

"I'm going to be there all summer on a study program."

Super shit. "That's a long time."

She laughed. "Not so long. I'll be back in the fall before the semester starts. Will you miss me?"

He shrugged. "Will you miss me?"

"Actually, yeah. I was hoping when I come back, maybe we can take another shot at this dating thing."

His balls tingled. "Really?"

"Yeah, silly. I still... you know."

His heart inflated. "What?"

She leaned forward and kissed him, but good. Her sweet mouth was so soft, it felt like sex heaven. Oh, the ideas he had for that mouth.

Meg pulled back and gave him a saucy smile. "That's so you don't forget me."

When she started to turn away, he reached out to clasp her wrist. With his other hand he reached into his pocket and pulled out the rose gold bracelet. Then he slowly fastened it around her wrist, maintaining eye contact with her the entire time. "That's so you don't forget *me.*"

She smiled and fingered the bracelet. "I couldn't." Then she turned and walked away, dragging his heart behind her.

It was going to be a long, cold summer.

CHAPTER 23

CARLOTTA SAT on the street behind the wheel of Hannah's borrowed van and watched Randolph pull his Mercedes SUV out of the driveway of the Buckhead house. She waited ten seconds, then followed him. Deep down she hoped he was going to the townhouse to work with Wes, or to golf with a buddy, or to meet with his attorney.

But his growing preoccupation told her something else was going on, and she wanted to know what.

He stopped to get coffee in a drive-through, which didn't seem suspicious on the surface—until she noticed two to-go cups being handed to him through the window. The knot in her stomach tightened, but she decided to see this through. She stayed two or three vehicles behind him.

When he left the coffee place, he drove to another residential area, this one newer than the neighborhood they lived in. The houses were bigger, the amenities nicer. When Randolph turned into the guard house of a particularly posh neighborhood, her heart sank lower. This was looking more and more like a personal visit to someone's residence. A lover? If so, she was a rich lover.

Or at least her husband was.

Carlotta hung back until he'd driven through the gate, then pulled the van alongside the guard house. A guy came strolling out dressed in security-chic garb.

She zoomed down the window and blasted him with a smile and

her best southern drawl. "Hi!"

"Hello. Can I help you?"

"Oh, gosh, yes, I could sure use your help. I was just in a little fender bender at the intersection back there." She gestured vaguely. "It was totally my fault—and the guy I hit said no big deal, but I feel terrible and I want to give him my insurance information." She held up a piece of pink paper. "I saw him pull in here—nice-looking older guy, Mercedes SUV. I think he said his name was Wren."

"Oh, yeah—he just went through."

"Well if you don't mind, I just want to buzz through, drop this off, and then I'll be right back out, in a flash." She blasted him with another smile.

He looked uncertain.

"Please—I'll only be two shakes because I'm running late for a nail appointment." She wiggled her fingers to boost her argument

He shrugged. "I guess it'll be okay. Mr. Wren went to see Marcy Lipscomb at 355 Elsier Street. Take the first right, then another right, and it's the white house on the left."

"Thank you so much."

She maintained her smile for the guard, but inside she was seething.

Randolph, it seemed, was up to his old tricks.

She waved as she drove through the gate, then followed his directions to the white house.

And what a house, she thought as she drove up. The woman had good taste, she'd give her that.

No class, apparently, but good taste.

Randolph's SUV was parked on the circular driveway in front of the expansive dwelling. He was just climbing out, armed with the two coffees. She hung back and watched him walk to the front door. When it opened, her stomach crimped. Marcy Lipscomb was the blonde from the club gala, the one Randolph had said he couldn't introduce her to because he'd forgotten her name. She was dressed beautifully and had a big smile for him. She took one of the coffees, and again Carlotta was struck by the familiarity of their body language. They had obviously spent quite a lot of time together.

Anger spurred her on. She pulled the van into the driveway behind the SUV, garnering the attention of both Randolph and his mistress. Carlotta put the van in park, then climbed out. When Randolph saw her, his shoulders fell. Determined to tell him what she thought of him, she strode forward. The couple stood frozen.

When she got close enough to see the trapped expression on her father's face, she held up her hands. "Are you going to introduce us, Dad?"

"Carlotta, this isn't what you probably think."

She gave a little laugh. "Really? You've been spending all this time away from the house, away from Mom, and apparently, you've been spending it here. So tell me, Dad, if this isn't what I think, then what is it?"

He sighed and gestured to the blonde. "This is Marcy Lipscomb. She's a real estate agent."

"Okay."

"And she helped me buy this house... for your mother... for all of us."

Carlotta blinked. "You bought another house?"

"I thought it would be better for your mother to be in a new place, where she wasn't reminded of our old life, and painful things."

"It's not just a house," Marcy offered with a smile. "It's customized for handicapped access—oversized doorways, ramps, and an elevator."

"For the day your mom had to be in a wheelchair," Randolph said.

"My husband is handicapped," Marcy said. "So it's become a little niche of mine."

Carlotta digested the information, and swallowed hard. "You

bought mom a house."

"That we could grow old in." He gave her a smile. "If things go as well with her surgery as I hope, we may not need the other features… at least not as soon as we might have otherwise."

"So this is where you've been going every day?"

He nodded. "The closing was the day of your mother's appointment, that's why I was late, I couldn't change it."

Carlotta's eyes welled. He'd bought it before he'd known that Valerie might get better.

Randolph handed his coffee to Marcy. "Give us a minute."

She nodded, then disappeared inside the house.

Carlotta was crying in earnest now. "I thought the worst of you."

"It's okay," he said, pulling her into his arms. "I can see how it might look, especially in light of my behavior when I was young and foolish."

"When the doctors said Mom might get better, I thought you seemed… angry."

"I was," he said, his voice breaking. "I was angry at myself. If I'd taken her to better doctors, maybe she could've been spared the last three years of going in and out of lucidity. Priscilla, too."

"You can't blame yourself for trusting the doctors, anyone would have. We have to keep looking forward."

He nodded, then pulled back. "I should've told you and Wes what I was doing with this house, but your mom has been like she is for so long, I guess I'm used to making decisions in a vacuum. I'll try to do better."

She nodded and sniffed mightily. "Me too. Wes and I talked about us all seeing a family therapist… what do you think?"

He smiled. "I think that's a good place to start." He clasped her hand for a squeeze. "Now, how about that tour?"

CHAPTER 24

"NEXT?"

Wes walked up the Emory University information window where a Calvin Klein model was stationed. "Uh, hi..." He looked at the guy's nametag. "Jamison."

Jamison gave Wes's holey jeans and T-shirt a once-over, then pulled back, as if to distance himself from discount clothing. "And what can I do for you?"

How about lose the attitude? "I'd like some information about admissions."

The guy gave a little eye roll. "You're going to have to be more specific."

"Uh, okay... how do I get in?"

Jamison's pursed his pretty mouth. "Which major?"

"I was thinking pre-med."

He gave a little head bobble as if he were holding back a laugh. Then he leaned forward and whispered, "Dude, no offense, but I think you're in the wrong place."

"I thought this was Emory Admissions information."

"It is."

"Okay, so what do I need to do to apply?"

The guy scoffed. "Well, first you need a fantastic high school resume and a great SAT score—and by great, I mean almost perfect. And letters of reference from alumni. What year are you?"

"I graduated two years ago."

He grunted. "A non-traditional student—that's going to be even harder." And he looked happy about it.

Wes bit down on his tongue. "Okay. Do I get admissions paperwork here?"

"Dude, I'll save you some time. You're not going to get into Emory. I mean, it's cute, this act of yours, but if you don't even know how to get into college, you shouldn't *be* in college."

He tasted blood. "Are you out of admissions forms?"

More attitude. *"No."*

"Then can I have one?"

Jamison sighed dramatically, then reached below the counter and came up with a three-inch thick folder. He plopped it on the counter with a thud, then slid it across to Wes. "Here you go, sport."

"Thanks a heap, Jamison." Wes took the file and walked back through the building, then out onto the campus, through manicured lawns, past attractive students who seemed to belong. The farther he walked, the more he felt Meg sliding away from him. He would never fit into her world.

When he passed a trash can, he stopped and dropped the admissions packet inside, then made his way back to the parking lot where Mouse sat in the Town Car, waiting.

The driver side window came down and Mouse grinned. "How'd it go?"

"Not so good," Wes said.

"What do you mean?"

"I don't think this is the place for me."

"You mean Emory?"

"I mean college."

"Just like that?"

"No. I've been thinking about it, and I just don't think I'm cut out for it."

Mouse made a thoughtful noise. "Well, if that's what you

think. You don't have to go to college to be successful—look at me."

Wes laughed, then realized Mouse hadn't meant it as a joke. "Oh... right. Yeah, I've got some other options I'm working. But thanks for the ride, man."

"No problem. Can I drop you somewhere?"

"Nah, I'm good."

"Okay, see you later."

Wes walked out of the parking lot with a particular destination in mind. A couple of blocks over, he approached a guy hanging out on a park bench and held up a cigarette. "Got a light?"

"Yeah." The guy pulled out a lighter.

"Got any O?"

The guy looked at him. "Got any cash?"

Wes pulled out a bill.

They made the exchange in three seconds and Wes walked away, turning the little baggy of pills over in his fingers. Just feeling the outline of them sent a zing up his arm.

His phone rang. He pulled it out to see Coop's name come up and connected the call. "Hey, man."

"Hi, Wes. I have to make a run to the hospital morgue, wondered if you wanted to go with me."

Randolph's disdain for the body moving gig reared in his mind. "Nah, man, I'm busy tonight."

"Okay, I'll catch you next time."

Wes ended the call and started to put away his phone, then punched in his dad's number.

Randolph answered on the first ring. "Hi, son. You coming over for dinner?"

"Not tonight," Wes said. "I just wanted to call and tell you I've made a decision... about your offer."

"And what have you decided?"

"Poker," he said. "I choose poker."

"Terrific," Randolph said, his voice ringing with parental

approval. "I'll take you over to the driving range soon and give you a tour of your new work digs."

"Sure thing," Wes said, then ended the call.

He turned the little baggy of pills over and over in his fingers.

CHAPTER 25

"THANKS FOR THE POSTCARD from Vegas," June Moody said.

Carlotta smiled. "You're welcome. I'm sorry it's taken me so long to stop by to say hello."

"You've been a little busy," June said, then she leaned on the bar. "How are you doing with all of this?"

"It depends on what day you ask me... but today is good." The door opened and Coop walked in. "Today is very good."

June smiled. "Won't argue with you there. Hi, Coop."

"Hi, June. This place is hopping. Business is good, huh?"

She nodded. "When the economy is bad, people drink and smoke cigars. And when the economy is good, people drink and smoke cigars more. What can I get you?"

"Seltzer water, please."

"Be right back."

Coop sat on the bar stool next to Carlotta. "Hello, you."

"Hi, there."

He gave her a nice kiss, then murmured. "Have you changed your mind?"

About sleeping over at his place. "No, sir."

He grinned. "Good." He looked past her and waved. "Hi, Rainie."

Carlotta turned to see Rainie Stephens walking down the stairs from the second floor lounge. The pretty redhead was known to keep company with Coop, so she hoped this wasn't going to be awkward.

"Hi, Coop… Carlotta."

"Hi, Rainie. How are you?"

Rainie nodded. "I'm good… you're just the person I wanted to see."

"Oh? About?"

"Talking your dad into doing a TV interview with me."

"He mentioned you'd asked about it. But he's gotten lots of offers."

"I'm sure he has. That's why I need you to talk to him for me." Her gaze flitted to Coop, then back. "I think you owe me one, don't you?"

Next to her, Coop shifted.

"I mean, I've kept things out of the paper to protect your family," Rainie said.

Carlotta dipped her chin. "I'll see what I can do."

"Thank you. It would be a huge get for me. It's the story of the year, and just keeps going."

"Oh? Any new developments on Walt Tully?"

"Not yet. No, I was talking about Liz Fischer."

Carlotta frowned. "What about Liz?"

"You haven't heard? Her court psych results are back, to determine if she's fit to stand trial."

"And?"

"The judge said no, she's not."

Carlotta scoffed. "How's that possible?"

"The pregnancy probably had a lot to do with it."

"Pregnancy?"

"It was a hysterical pregnancy… she's not having a baby—it was all in her head."

Carlotta went completely still. "Liz… isn't… pregnant?"

"Nope."

Jack wasn't having a baby, wasn't tied to Liz anymore. She felt light-headed from the revelation. So many things had just been undone, for the better. A child wouldn't be born in prison, to an unstable mother and reluctant father.

And Jack was free.

She could sense Coop watching her, gauging her reaction. She tried to school her face, but she could feel a flush burning its way up her neck. Soon her face was on fire. "Excuse me," she said, pushing to her feet a little unsteadily. "I need to powder my nose."

She made it to the bathroom, and sank down on a couch. She pressed her palms into her eyes to keep the tears at bay. She couldn't go back out there and let Coop see she was upset about this. Jack's words about things he hadn't told her kept playing over in her head.

What if he did love her, and now he was unencumbered to tell her?

Then she smacked her palm against her forehead once, twice, three times. The man had been free to tell her how he felt about her for a long while before the mention of a baby, and he hadn't. When would she ever learn, Jack Terry was never going to commit to her?

She had a good thing going with Coop—she was starting to fall in love with him. He was so good to her, and to her family. He would love her and take care of her, the way her dad was taking care of her mother. She could see that now.

She wanted this... she wanted permanence... she wanted Coop.

Happiness flooded her chest, confirming her decision. She exhaled a cleansing breath, then walked back out into the bar, looking forward to spending the night in Coop's arms.

But his bar stool was empty, and Rainie was gone. June was wiping the counter, looking dour.

"Where's Coop?"

"He left."

Carlotta blinked. "Left... as in, not coming back?"

"Right. With, um, Rainie."

June slid a folded piece of paper toward her. "He asked me to give you this."

Carlotta frowned and opened the note.

Carlotta, I can't do this anymore. Coop

CHAPTER 26

"PRISSY, STOP wriggling," Carlotta said behind her new phone positioned on books stacked on a table. "Wes, scoot back. Mom, smile. Dad, look this way. Jack, stay. Okay, five seconds, here I come."

Carlotta ran to wedge between Wes and Prissy. "Cheese," they chorused, and the flash went off.

They all laughed and relaxed. Finally, a family portrait, no stuffy clothes or pose, but all of them as they were.

"Okay," Carlotta announced, "now it's time for the long-awaited Wren family Christmas." She gestured to the shabby, sad little metallic tree they'd transplanted from the townhouse to the Buckhead house. "Putting up this tree was one of the last things we all did together as a family before Mom and Dad had to leave. Wes made me leave it up all these years and wait to open the gifts until we could all be together. So... Merry Christmas!"

"Merry Christmas!" her Mom and Dad chorused, holding hands.

She was overjoyed to see them re-dedicating themselves to their marriage. Valerie was so much improved after the shunt had been inserted, Carlotta was starting to forget the other version of her mother. This edition of her mother was like before, only better—she was happy, and sober. And Randolph seemed determined to

STEPHANIE BOND

get things right this time. When he looked at Valerie, his adoration was evident.

"This is so exciting," her mother said. "I can't even remember what I wrapped up for you two."

Wes passed out the small gifts, the paper of which was a little worse for wear. There was one gift each for her and Wesley, and two for Randolph and Valerie from them. First, Wes opened his package, and his eyes lit up. "It's a watch."

"Oh... it was my father's watch," Valerie said, smiling. "It's a family heirloom, actually, because it was his father's. I remember now that I wanted you to have it, Wes. I was so worried it would be seized along with our other assets."

"I love it, Mom," Wes said, then gave her a big hug and kiss and strapped it on his wrist.

"Carlotta, you go next," Valerie urged.

Carlotta tore open the paper to find a small gray velvet jeweler's box. She opened it and gasped to see the piece of gold jewelry inside. "It's a necklace. Oh, it's beautiful." She held it up, admiring the filigree of the large oval pendant. "Wait, it's a locket. And Mom, you put a note inside the box... it says, To Carlotta, I want you to have a picture of your father to hold near your heart."

She smiled, then opened the locket, but frowned at the picture of a man she didn't recognize. "But this isn't a picture of Daddy." She turned the locket toward them so they could laugh at the mistake.

But instead of laughing, the color had drained from their faces.

"What?" she asked, looking back and forth.

Randolph was glaring at Valerie, tears in his eyes. "How could you?"

Valerie shook her head. "I forgot... I was so angry with you over Liz... I completely forgot I did this."

Randolph stood and strode from the room.

"What's going on?" Carlotta asked her mother. "Who is this man?"

Valerie looked stricken, then visibly pulled herself together and lifted her chin. "Carlotta... he's your real father."

Carlotta's world tilted, then fell on its face.

-The End-

A NOTE FROM THE AUTHOR

Thank you so very much for reading 9 BODIES ROLLING! I hope you enjoyed this book as much as I enjoyed researching and writing it. No matter how many projects take me away from Body Movers, I'm always happy to come back to these characters I know and love. Since so many story lines were tied up in 8 BODIES IS ENOUGH, I wanted this book to be more about the emotional fallout of those endpoints... and to reset the characters a bit. In book ten, Carlotta will be spring-boarding from a new place emotionally! (Yes, I'll be writing more Body Movers books— Carlotta and the gang still have lots of adventures ahead!)

If you enjoyed 9 BODIES ROLLING and feel inclined to leave a review at your favorite online bookseller, I would appreciate it very much. Reviews help my books find new readers, which means I can keep writing new stories! Plus I always want to know what my readers are thinking. Thank you for your support— without readers like you, there wouldn't be a Body Movers series!

Are you signed up to receive notices of my future book releases? If not, please visit www.stephaniebond.com and enter your email address. I won't flood you with emails and I'll never share or sell your address, and you can unsubscribe at any time. While you're on my website, check out the FAQs page for more information about the history and the future of the Body Movers series.

Thanks again for your time and interest, and for telling your friends about my books. As long as you keep reading, I'll keep writing!

Happy reading!

Stephanie Bond

OTHER WORKS BY STEPHANIE BOND

Humorous romantic mysteries:
COMEBACK GIRL—*Home is where the hurt is.*
TEMP GIRL—*Change is good... but not great.*
COMA GIRL—*You can learn a lot when people think you aren't listening.*
TWO GUYS DETECTIVE AGENCY—*Even Victoria can't keep a secret from us...*
OUR HUSBAND—*Hell hath no fury like three women scorned!*
KILL THE COMPETITION—*There's only one sure way to the top...*
I THINK I LOVE YOU—*Sisters share everything in their closets...including the skeletons.*
GOT YOUR NUMBER—*You can run, but your past will eventually catch up with you.*
WHOLE LOTTA TROUBLE—*They didn't plan on getting caught...*
IN DEEP VOODOO—*A woman stabs a voodoo doll of her ex, and then he's found murdered!*
VOODOO OR DIE—*Another voodoo doll, another untimely demise...*
BUMP IN THE NIGHT—*a short mystery*

***Body Movers* series:**
PARTY CRASHERS (full-length prequel)
BODY MOVERS
2 BODIES FOR THE PRICE OF 1
3 MEN AND A BODY
4 BODIES AND A FUNERAL
5 BODIES TO DIE FOR
6 KILLER BODIES
6 ½ BODY PARTS (novella)
7 BRIDES FOR SEVEN BODIES
8 BODIES IS ENOUGH
9 BODIES ROLLING

Romances:
ALMOST A FAMILY—*Fate gave them a second chance at love...*
LICENSE TO THRILL—*She's between a rock and a hard body...*
STOP THE WEDDING!—*If anyone objects to this wedding, speak now...*
THREE WISHES—*Be careful what you wish for!*

The Southern Roads series:
BABY, I'M YOURS (novella)
BABY, DRIVE SOUTH
BABY, COME HOME
BABY, DON'T GO
BABY, I'M BACK (novella)
BABY, HOLD ON (novella)
BABY, IT'S YOU (novella)

Nonfiction:
GET A LIFE! 8 STEPS TO CREATE YOUR OWN LIFE LIST—*a short how-to for mapping out your personal life list!*
YOUR PERSONAL FICTION-WRITING COACH: *365 Days of Motivation & Tips to Write a Great Book!*

ABOUT THE AUTHOR

Stephanie Bond was seven years deep into a corporate career in computer programming and pursuing an MBA at night when an instructor remarked she had a flair for writing and suggested she submit material to academic journals. But Stephanie was more interested in writing fiction—more specifically, romance and mystery novels. After writing in her spare time for two years, she sold her first manuscript; after selling ten additional projects to two publishers, she left her corporate job to write fiction full-time. To-date, Stephanie has more than eighty published novels to her name, including the popular BODY MOVERS humorous mystery series, and STOP THE WEDDING!, a romantic comedy adapted into a movie for the Hallmark Channel. Stephanie lives in Atlanta, where she is probably working on a story at this very moment. For more information on Stephanie's books, visit www.stephaniebond.com.

COPYRIGHT INFORMATION

Made in the USA
Middletown, DE
12 September 2018